MIKE RO

NUJ
NATIONAL UNION
OF JOURNALISTS

MEMBER: MICHAEL ROFONE

Mike Rofone

CARMEL CRAWFORD
CLARE DOWLING

BLACKWATER PRESS

First Published in 1996 by Blackwater Press,
Unit 7/8 Broomhill Business Park, Tallaght, Dublin 24,
Ireland.

Printed at the Press of the Publishers.

Editor: Deirdre Whelan
Assistant Editor: Zoë O'Connor
Design/Graphics: Philip Ryan
Illustration: Aileen Caffrey

ISBN 0 86121 827 2
British Library Cataloguing-in-Publication Data.
A catalogue record for this book is available from the
British Library. Crawford/Dowling. Mike Rofone

CONTENTS

CHAPTER 1

Indie Johnson was grounded.

Earlier that day, it was discovered that the bicycle shed at the back of the school had somehow or other been sprayed with graffiti. Bright red letters and symbols now decorated the newly-painted shed.

"Desecration!" the headmistress cried.

"Mindless vandalism!" the teachers roared.

"Wanton destruction!" the parents fumed.

And they all set about looking for the culprit. But nobody seemed to have seen a thing.

Eventually, the school caretaker was consulted. He hadn't seen a thing either – he'd just locked the school gates after the last child had left. At this, the headmistress, the teachers and the parents held their breaths suspiciously – who exactly was the last child out of the school?

"Indie Johnson," the caretaker announced.

And so Indie Johnson immediately became the chief suspect in the case of the bike shed graffiti.

"But I didn't do it!" he howled in indignation. "I was only collecting my bike!"

But unfortunately, Indie Johnson has one of those faces that looks like trouble. Adults are immediately wary of his bright, inquisitive eyes and his jaunty walk. They distrust the way he wears his baseball cap backwards and the fact that his hair is far too long for an eleven-year-old. Frankly, he makes them nervous.

The result is that Indie is always a prime suspect in any wrong-doing, when, in fact, he's usually entirely innocent.

"You believe me, Mum, don't you?" he asked his mother that evening.

She hesitated, not answering. Indie was shocked – she doubted him! He turned to his father for support.

"Dad! You know I wouldn't do something like that!"

But his father didn't quite meet his eyes. Indie was doubly shocked. An outlaw in his own home!

"Indie," his mother said carefully, "it's not that we don't believe you. But you do have a habit of always being in the wrong place at the wrong time."

"But Mum!"

"Just a second, Indie!" his father said sternly. "We're not saying that you did it. But how many times now have you been suspected of trouble?"

Lots of time, Indie knew. He had the bad luck to be cycling past Mr Ryan's car just before it was discovered that someone had let the air out of the tyres. It was Indie's football that had been found in Mrs O'Brien's back garden, just after her window got broken – never mind that he'd lost that football months before. And who happened to be in the vicinity when one of old Mrs Mulcahy's rhubarb tarts went missing from her window ledge? Indie, of course. She hadn't listened when he'd protested that he was allergic to rhubarb.

But his parents had usually believed him. Up until now, at least.

"Sorry, Indie, but we're going to have to get to the bottom of this one," his father said. His mother nodded in agreement. Indie knew he was defeated.

He was also grounded. Banished to his bedroom for the evening, deprived of TV, phone calls from his friends and chocolate chip ice cream.

"And I didn't even do it!" he fumed in frustration to his empty bedroom. He flung himself on his bed and spent a pleasant hour dreaming up all kinds of horrific punishments for the real culprit, if he or she was ever found.

"Bedtime, Indie!" his mother called from the hall.

Indie grew angry. He decided that if he was going to be painted as a black sheep, then he'd *act* like a black sheep. The first bit of misbehaviour would be his refusal to go to bed.

"Sure Mum," he lied, before settling himself down in front of his computer. Defiantly, he keyed in his password and waited. Bingo! He was on the Internet.

Indie had been one of the first kids on his street to get hooked up to the Net. In fact, at about the time when the bike shed graffiti was discovered, he'd been busily doing his homework with the help of the Net – a geography project, which he had brightened up with a great big colourful map of Africa he'd downloaded and printed out from his computer. Of course, he didn't just use the Net for homework. There was plenty of fun to be had at the touch of a key – books to be read, games to be played and friends to be e-mailed.

But right now, it was too late to e-mail any of his friends. He decided to look for amusement on one of the many kids' chatlines.

Busily, he hopped from one to another, looking for an interesting conversation. But his heart wasn't in it this evening, not after the bike shed incident. He was wondering how to trap the real culprit of the graffiti when he saw it out of the corner of his eye... a foot. A foot?

He immediately clicked backwards to the chatline where he'd seen this foot. But it was gone.

He blinked rapidly, wondering whether there was something wrong with his eyesight. He hoped he wouldn't have to get glasses.

There it was again! That foot! And there was a gloved hand, and above that, the side of a head. Somebody was trying to conceal themselves by the side of his computer screen!

"Caught you!" Indie muttered to the computer,

wondering if this was some new Net game he hadn't heard of.

But to his amazement, his computer spoke back to him. Or, rather, hissed.

"Why don't you be quiet! I'm on a stake-out!"

Indie jumped in fright. Either he or his computer had gone completely barmy.

"Pssstt!" The voice came again, from the side of the screen. "Is the coast clear?"

What coast? Indie quickly looked around his bedroom, but could see nothing alarming.

"Eh, I think so," he said, feeling very foolish talking to his computer.

Then the half-concealed foot at the side of his screen took a giant step inwards. The gloved hand followed, then the head, and the person who had been hiding out by the side of his computer now stood slap bang in the middle of the screen.

Only, it wasn't a person at all. It was a microphone. A microphone with legs. And a head. And a mouth, which now opened and yawned loudly and rather rudely.

This microphone reached forward, stuck its hand out, firmly grabbed Indie's hand and shook it vigorously.

"Pleased to meet ya," he drawled. "The name's Rofone. Mike Rofone."

He let go of Indie's hand and grinned.

Indie was astounded. "How did you do that?"

"Do what?"

"Shake my hand? Through a computer screen?"

Mike Rofone grinned cheekily. "That's a trade secret."

Indie was more confused. What trade?

His question was answered as Mike reached into his pocket and whipped out a badge. The badge was a little tattered around the edges, but Indie could make out a small photo of Mike.

In smaller letters, the badge announced that he was a journalist.

"I'm with *The Daily Rap*," Mike announced, putting the badge away.

"*The Daily Rap*? What's that?"

"It's an American newspaper," Mike said proudly. "I'm its star reporter."

This all seemed incredible to Indie.

"B-but you're a MICROPHONE!" he stuttered.

Mike looked highly indignant. "Of course I'm a microphone! You think I don't know who I am?"

Indie dumbly shook his head.

Mike did a little strut across the computer screen.

"I might be a microphone, but I'm one of the hottest reporters around! I've got more scoops than any other reporter you care to name. Ask anybody."

Indie still looked baffled. Mike Rofone plonked himself down on the side of the screen and crossed his legs casually.

"Remember the two viruses that surfaced last year and threatened to destroy the entire Net system?"

Indie nodded, his eyes growing round. He'd kept his computer turned off for an entire month in case the viruses got into it.

Mike leaned forward cockily.

"Well, I caught one of those viruses. Blackrattler was his name."

Indie looked at Mike in awe. "You did?"

Mike shrugged modestly. "Yep. He's inside for life."

Indie looked a little scared. "What happened the other virus? Is he still around?"

Mike shrugged solemnly. "Nobody knows. Viper Virus, he calls himself. He was the brains behind the entire outfit, but he let Blackrattler take the rap. Then he just disappeared off the face of the earth. But I'll catch him one day."

"What other scoops did you get?" Indie asked eagerly.

Mike shrugged modestly, as though it were against his nature to boast. But he did anyway. "Well, I rescued those virtual tourists who were stranded when the Net broke down. And I caught those shoplifters who were stealing stuff from the One Stop Shop on the Web."

Indie was amazed. "I think I remember reading about that. In the newspapers."

"Yep. I wrote those articles."

"Wow. You're something else."

"Oh stop," Mike said bashfully. Then he seemed to remember something and scowled at Indie.

"And I was just about to crack my latest scoop, when you, young man, ruined it all!"

Indie was by now flabbergasted.

"By messing up my stake-out!" Mike spat, pointing an accusing finger at Indie.

This was all too much for Indie. Here he was again, being blamed for something he didn't do. It just wasn't fair.

"I didn't ruin anything!" he retaliated. "You're just lousy at hiding!"

Mike Rofone was speechless. He looked at Indie hard. Indie glared back, determined to stand up for himself for once. Then, to his surprise, Mike shrugged casually, and nodded.

"You're right. I never was much good at hiding. Sorry."

Indie deflated. He felt a little respect growing for Mike Rofone. When adults eventually discovered that Indie wasn't the culprit in some mischief or other, they usually didn't bother apologising to him. But Mike had.

"Apology accepted," he said properly. His curiosity grew. "Who are you looking for?"

Mike Rofone shot a furtive glance over his left shoulder, then his right, as if he expected somebody to be creeping up on him this very minute.

"Can I trust you?" he asked.

Indie nodded.

Mike looked at him for a long moment, as if measuring him up.

"What's your name?" he suddenly asked.

"Indie."

"Right, Indie. Hold on tight."

"Hold on tight? What—"

But Indie was cut off in mid-sentence as Mike casually reached through the computer screen and grabbed the front of his t-shirt. Suddenly, he was lifted clean out of his chair. His stomach flipped as he felt himself flying through the air. Then, a gentle plopping noise, as though he were being sucked through a liquid bubble.

The next thing he knew, he was lying flat on his back, on solid ground.

He looked around, confused. He seemed to be lying on a vast white floor that stretched for miles and miles in every direction as far as the eye could see. To his right, he could see his bedroom. But it looked very small and kind of distorted, as if it were behind some kind of mirror, or glass... glass? It was then that Indie realised that he was inside his own computer.

"Cool, huh?" Mike asked.

Indie looked up to see Mike standing over him.

"Where am I?"

Mike grinned. "You're on the Net."

Things just keep getting weirder and weirder, thought Indie. He got to his feet slowly and looked around, amazed. He was actually on the Internet!

"Get down quick!" hissed Mike, who took a dramatic dive to the floor. Indie quickly followed suit.

"What's up?"

"Sssshhh! We don't want to scare him off!"

"Scare who?"

But Mike didn't answer. Instead, he started to crawl along the ground on his belly, slowly and stealthily. Indie crawled after him.

Suddenly, a seedy-looking man in a dirty raincoat crept out from where he'd been hiding. He looked around furtively.

"Oi! You come back here now, you scum!" Mike roared. The man jumped in fright. Then he scowled over his shoulder.

"Sure, Mike," he said sarcastically. "What do you think I am, stupid?"

"Yes."

The man scowled some more. Then, without warning, he whirled around and sprinted away, as if for his life. In seconds, he'd disappeared over the white horizon.

Mike Rofone hopped about in fury. "I've lost him! I've lost the creep!"

Indie prudently waited until he'd calmed down.

"Who was that?"

Mike continued to glare at the horizon where the man had disappeared. "That was Jason Ratz," he said through clenched teeth. "He calls himself a reporter too, but his newspaper, *The Rattler*, is nothing more than a cheap rag."

Indie was surprised at Mike's vehement tone and the look of disgust on his face. He wondered what Ratz had done to him.

"Is he out to steal your story or something?"

Mike laughed, but it wasn't a particularly pleasant sound. "Whatever Ratz is up to, he isn't reporting. That'd be too much like hard work to him. His kind, they can barely heave themselves out of the gutter in the mornings."

Indie was now intrigued. "What's he doing then?"

But Mike was now business-like. "Time enough for explanations later. Right now, I've got to get back to the newspaper office and tell Mr Broadhead – he's my editor –

that Ratz has disappeared. We'll have to come up with another plan."

Mike set off at a fast run across the screen. Soon, he too disappeared over the horizon.

It was then that it dawned on Indie that he had no idea how to get out of his computer and back into his bedroom.

"Mike! Mike Rofone!" he shouted urgently. But there was no reply.

He sank down onto the ground again, wondering what on earth he was going to do. He could phone his Mum he supposed, but there didn't appear to be a phone box anywhere in the vicinity. In fact, there didn't appear to be anything at all except endless white space. Indie felt as though he were floating inside a huge milk bottle with no way of getting out...

"Ready?"

Indie almost jumped out of his skin. Mike stood over him expectantly. He held a six pack of cola. Indie felt so relieved that his knees went weak.

"Where were you?" he managed to squeak.

Mike looked at him curiously. "I left my cola over by my stake-out spot. Hey... you didn't think I'd just leave you, did you?"

"Hey. No way," Indie immediately blustered, imitating Mike.

Mike smiled at him mischievously. "Wanna come to my newspaper office for a quick visit?"

Indie's eyes gleamed. "Sure. Where is it?"

Mike grabbed him with one hand, and with the other, reached out through Indie's computer screen and tapped a few commands into the keyboard.

"You're about to be e-mailed," he announced.

And with that, they were lifted high into the air and sucked at speed through the layers of white, as if by a giant hoover.

CHAPTER 2
●●●●●●●●●●●●●

Mike Rofone had a nervous feeling in the pit of his belly. He always got nervous when he sniffed a good story in the air, just waiting to be investigated and published. But today he was just a little too nervous. He had a bad feeling about this story.

"I've got a bad feeling about this one," he announced. He was anxiously pacing the floor in the middle of the newspaper offices of *The Daily Rap*.

"We know. You've told us about your bad feelings at least ten times already," huffed Mr Broadhead.

Mr Broadhead, editor of *The Daily Rap*, was reclining in his custom-built leather swivel chair, which was ideal for snoozing. And boy, did Mr Broadhead like to snooze. Frequently, he had to be woken by a member of staff when it was time to go home, where he snoozed until bedtime. In fact, he was feeling a little sleepy right now... forty winks certainly wouldn't go astray...

"MR BROADHEAD!"

Mr Broadhead jerked awake with a loud snort and looked around wildly.

"What? What?"

Mike looked at him impatiently. "We've got a hot story here, and I'd appreciate it if you'd stay awake!"

Mr Broadhead made a huge effort to sit up straight and look business-like. He cast a stern eye over the newspaper office, making sure that everybody was busy. They were. Reporters bent over their desks reporting, editors editing and secretaries typing.

Satisfied, he turned back to Mike. It was then that he noticed the boy standing beside Mike.

"Who are you?"

Mike turned to Indie and rolled his eyes in exasperation. He'd already introduced Mr Broadhead to Indie ten minutes ago. Really, sometimes Mr Broadhead was just too much.

"This is Indie, all right? He's just here to see what a newspaper office looks like."

"Hello Indie," said Mr Broadhead. "Pleased to meet you. I'm..."

"Mr Broadhead," Mike prompted helpfully.

"Am I? Yes, yes of course I am," said Mr Broadhead, who didn't look at all sure.

Indie shook Mr Broadhead's hand, then looked around again.

"Where are we?"

"Huh? In the newspaper office," Mr Broadhead said.

"I know, but where is it?"

"Florida."

Wow, Indie thought. He was in Florida. In a real live newspaper office!

He'd never been in one before, and couldn't get over the hustle and bustle, with people shouting and computers printing and new story leads coming in by phone every two minutes. He decided on the spot that he wanted to be a reporter when he left school.

His attention was grabbed by Mike Rofone, who had stopped dramatically in the middle of the floor.

"You want to know why I've got a bad feeling?"

Mr Broadhead and Indie nodded in unison. Mike lowered his voice.

"Whatever Jason Ratz was up to earlier today, he's not alone. He hasn't got the brains to carry any scam off on his own. It makes me nervous."

For the first time, Mr Broadhead looked totally alert and serious.

"I just found out what he was doing on the Net today, Mike."

Mike Rofone stood stock still, his reporter's nose going into overdrive. He'd known all along there was something fishy going on.

"He was carrying a disk, Mike. A computer disk that he didn't want you to get your hands on."

"A disk?" Mike looked baffled.

Mr Broadhead elaborated dramatically. "Jason Ratz is in the thick of an evil plot involving subliminal messages on the Internet!"

Indie's eyes grew round. He'd heard all about subliminal messages – hidden messages that you can't see but that affect you anyway.

Mike Rofone had his notebook out, and started firing questions at Mr Broadhead.

"These messages – are they on the Net now?"

"No. The messages are on that disk Ratz was carrying. But I reckon Ratz and his gang are planning to use them soon."

Mike Rofone groaned heavily.

"It gets worse, Mike," Mr Broadhead said, shaking his shaggy head mournfully. "They're targeting kids' chatlines on the Net with these messages. I think they're aiming to brainwash kids all over the world!"

Mike Rofone was astounded. The sheer enormity of the plan, the consequences for children everywhere... it was unthinkable. Again, he started pacing furiously, his mind going in ten different directions.

"Any more information on who else is in this gang?" he asked Mr Broadhead.

"No," Mr Broadhead said quickly. A little too quickly.

"You sure?" Mike asked suspiciously.

Mr Broadhead's eyes slid to the desk. "Well, there's a couple of rumours flying around."

Mike grew more suspicious. He motioned for Mr Broadhead to continue. Mr Broadhead seemed to grow a little paler. His voice was hushed.

"I heard from a very reliable source that the leader of the gang is... Viper Virus."

Mike Rofone – who doesn't shock easily – was shocked. "Viper Virus?"

"Yes," Mr Broadhead shivered, as do most decent people when Viper Virus's name is mentioned.

Mike shivered too. When he'd busted Viper's outfit last year and got his buddy Blackrattler arrested, Viper had vowed that Mike would come to a horrible end.

But then Viper had vanished and Mike had almost forgotten about him.

"So, he's back," Mike muttered to himself.

"And that's not all, Mike," Mr Broadhead added. "This disk that Ratz had on him today – word is that he got it from Blackrattler, who's been secretly working on it in prison for the last year. He smuggled it out to Ratz via a messenger."

"Blackrattler's in on this too?"

"Yep. But one of the prison guards caught on to him and he's in solitary confinement now. He won't be causing any more trouble for a long time."

"Too late!" Mike groaned. "He got the disk out, didn't he? To Viper Virus of all people. See? I told you I had a bad feeling about this story!"

Mr Broadhead looked crafty. "I can always assign it to somebody else."

Mike looked highly insulted, as Mr Broadhead knew he would.

"No way," Mike said meanly, his eyes narrowing. "Viper and I have some unfinished business."

Wow, he thought, I sound just like somebody from a movie.

"Excuse me?" said a small voice.

Both Mike and Mr Broadhead looked up to see Indie standing between them.

"I know I'm only an amateur at this reporting game, but it seems to me that if you can get hold of that disk, then you'll have stopped them in their tracks."

"The thing is," Mr Broadhead said, "the disk is probably with Viper now and we don't know where he's hiding."

Mr Broadhead and Mike fell silent, lost in thought. Indie was trying to take it all in, his face flushed with excitement. He still couldn't believe he was actually in Florida. Wait until he told his Mum...

"Uh-oh."

Mike looked up. "What?"

Indie looked miserable. "I've just remembered. I'm supposed to be home in my bedroom. I'm grounded."

Mr Broadhead looked fondly into the distance. "I remember when I was grounded. Back in 1953. You see, there was this girl..."

Mike Rofone threw his eyes to heaven. He'd heard the story of how Mr Broadhead was grounded at least ten million times.

"Another time, Mr Broadhead, eh?" he said kindly, before turning to Indie.

"What has you grounded?"

"Oh, someone painted graffiti onto the school shed. I got the blame. And I'm going to be in more trouble when they find out I've been gone for hours," Indie finished.

Mike slung a sympathetic arm around Indie. "Listen. Time doesn't move the same on the Net as it does in the real world."

"What?"

"It moves much faster. Your parents probably won't even miss you."

Indie felt slightly better.

"How are you going to catch Viper and Ratz?" he asked, just to get off the subject of his parents.

Mike stroked his chin thoughtfully. "I don't know, but give me a minute."

He let his mind wander around the possibilities, play with theories and construct various schemes, all of which took him only a minute or two. It has to be pointed out, Mike has a marvellous mind.

"I think I've got a plan," he quietly announced.

Mr Broadhead was glad. *He* didn't have one. In fact, he had difficulty remembering what they were even discussing. Then, thankfully, it all came back to him.

"What's the plan?"

Mike Rofone grew excited.

"They're going to put these messages out on the Net, right? On kids' chatlines?"

Mr Broadhead nodded vigorously. Mike leaned closer.

"So, what I do is get on the chatlines to see if I can spot these messages – anything unusual at all – then *you*, Mr Broadhead, can have a go at tracing their origin!"

Mr Broadhead hadn't quite grasped it all yet. "And?"

"And that should lead us straight to Viper Virus and his merry band of villains!"

"Brilliant!" Mr Broadhead said, looking at Mike in awe.

"Do I get a pay rise?" Mike shot.

"No way."

"I'm leaving to go to another paper!" Mike threatened.

"They couldn't afford you."

"You can't afford me!"

"Next month, okay?" Mr Broadhead grumbled. Give a reporter an inch and they take a mile, he thought morosely. He hadn't a clue what that actually meant, but it sounded good.

"Okay Indie, saddle up!" Mike said, rubbing his hands together enthusiastically.

"I'm going with you?" Indie said hopefully.

Mike made a little face. "Sorry. I meant I was taking you home."

Indie hesitated. He didn't want to be left out. "Can't I help? Maybe get on a chatline and look for these messages?"

"No. Too risky," Mr Broadhead said sternly.

"But—"

"No! Sorry, Indie, but it's just too dangerous. We'll keep you posted though, won't we, Mike?"

"Sure," said Mike, before hopping energetically on to the desk. In a flash, he'd jumped into Mr Broadhead's computer screen and was waiting for Indie.

"Bye, Mr Broadhead," Indie mumbled, hating to leave.

But Mr Broadhead was already busily at work. Indie felt a hand on his arm and suddenly, he was whipped into the computer screen and back onto the Net. Seconds later, he was spat out into his own bedroom, in Dublin, Ireland, where he landed in his chair in front of his own computer.

Already, Mike Rofone was preparing to zoom off across the Net again in pursuit of Ratz and Viper Virus.

"Mike? You'll let me know how it's going?"

"Sure," Mike said and, with a cheerful wave, disappeared from sight.

Indie stared at his blank computer screen, feeling lonely all of a sudden. But not for long. His bedroom door was hurled open and his mother stood there, arms folded ominously over her chest. Behind her stood his father. He looked equally annoyed.

Indie decided to come clean. "I'm sorry. I know I've been gone for hours and hours…"

At this, his parents exchanged puzzled glances. "You've only been gone about fifteen minutes," his mother said.

So it was true then, what Mike had said about time moving faster on the Net.

"But the point is not how long you've been gone," his father said, very annoyed now. "The point is you were told to stay in your bedroom!"

"I know, but I've been to Florida!"

More puzzled glances from his parents.

"It's true! And I met Mr Broadhead – he runs *The Daily Rap* – and you see we were trying to come up with a plan to catch Ratz and Viper Virus..."

His parents now grew alarmed. Florida? *The Daily Rap*? Viper Virus?

"I think he's been using that Internet thing far too much," his mother murmured to his father, who nodded in agreement.

The next thing, Indie found himself tucked up in bed with a stern warning not to budge until morning, while his father sailed out the door with his computer.

Mike Rofone was bleary-eyed.

"One more and I'm gonna call it a night," he promised himself. He'd visited close on fifty kids' chatlines looking for the subliminal messages. But not a sausage. Nothing but kids chatting and having a good time.

Mr Broadhead had gone home an hour ago. He'd tried to persuade Mike to do the same.

"Come on, Mike, you have to get some rest."

But Mike was like a terrier with a bone when it came to a scoop. He could lie in wait for days on end if it came to it.

"Right," he said wearily, as he arrived on his fifty-first chatline.

He broke open a cola and started to scan the lines of text. He was so tired that it swam in front of his eyes.

And it wasn't as if he even knew what he was looking for.

You can't see subliminal messages, that was the whole point. And Mike would bet a year's supply of cola that Viper Virus was clever enough to be subtle about the whole thing.

Hello – what was that? Mike's eyes narrowed. There, in the middle of the text, was a very peculiar message.

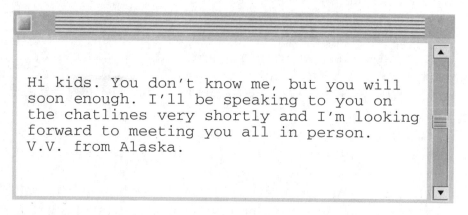

```
Hi kids. You don't know me, but you will
soon enough. I'll be speaking to you on
the chatlines very shortly and I'm looking
forward to meeting you all in person.
V.V. from Alaska.
```

VV? It could only mean one person, Mike decided – Viper Virus! And he'd just given himself away, by saying he was from Alaska! Catching Viper Virus was going to be easier than he'd thought!

As Mike prepared to e-mail himself to Alaska, he couldn't stop the growing doubt in his mind.

It was all too easy. Viper giving his initials, then letting slip where he lived. Mike knew that Viper was much brighter than that.

Maybe it was a red herring, designed to throw him off the trail. But he couldn't just ignore it, could he?

"Anyway, I've never been to Alaska," he said with false cheer, just before he was lifted into the air and propelled along the Superhighway.

CHAPTER 3

The dungeons were as black as night. Eerie. Noiseless.

Then, the heavy air swished, and Viper Virus plunged downwards from where he'd been hanging upside-down from a rafter. He landed gracefully on the filthy floor and stretched his bat wings luxuriously. He didn't bother turning on a light. Viper's kind can see in the dark.

"Come along my pretties! Dinnertime!" he shrieked, his voice high-pitched and unearthly.

He waited, but there wasn't a sound. So, he thought nastily, they were hiding from him.

"Come out NOW!" he trilled, an edge to his voice.

He cocked an ear and listened. Ah, the patter of tiny feet.

From the darkest corners of the dungeons they came running. Seven huge black sewer rats, one meaner than the other. Viper's pet rats.

"And how are we today, my lovelies?" he crooned.

The rats were starving. They'd had nothing to eat since yesterday except a few spiders. Their beady eyes fixed firmly on the lump of mouldy cheese in Viper's hand.

"And did we sleep well? Hmmm?" Viper teased, as he ever so slowly shaved off a tiny portion of the cheese. The rats, dying for the cheese, wished that Viper would just shut up and give it to them. But they knew better than to display such impatience. They'd had personal experience of Viper's awful temper.

"I must say, I slept very well indeed," Viper mused. "Today is D-Day, my pets! Today, the children of this world will be mine, all mine!"

A tiny crumb of cheese fell to the floor, and the largest of the rats impulsively darted forward and gobbled it up.

Viper, furious at this impertinence, hurled the rat halfway across the dungeons with a flick of his left wing.

"Wait your turn!" he bellowed. The rat picked itself up and crawled back, cowering submissively.

"As I was saying before I was so RUDELY interrupted," Viper continued, with a vicious look at the rat, "today, my subliminal messages will turn the world's children into my personal army. And do you know what happens after that? Do you, my darlings?"

The rats shook their heads in unison and tried to look interested.

"After that, it's only one short step to taking over the entire population! I will soon be world dictator!" He savoured this thought for a moment. Then his mood turned nasty.

"I'll show them. The people who have been out to ruin my career and destroy me! The day of reckoning will come!" he snarled.

The rats were in despair. Viper appeared to have forgotten all about the cheese. One of them grew bold, and squeaked appealingly. Viper came out of his trance and looked down.

"Ah. The cheese!" he said finally. The rats grinned and nodded and scraped the ground.

Viper took the piece of cheese he'd cut off and waved it tantalisingly in the air.

"And are we hungry? Yes?" he murmured gently.

The rats salivated and looked at him imploringly.

"Good. Unfortunately, so am I." With a horrible cackle, Viper popped the cheese into his own mouth.

The rats were livid. They darted forward, hissing and spitting viciously at Viper. Viper opened his bat wings and hissed and spat back. The rats, terrified, swiftly retreated into the darkness.

Viper laughed and laughed with glee. He loved teasing the

rats. He did it at least twice a day. And the rats, silly things, they never learned.

"AAAHHHH!" Viper suddenly roared in pain, and clutched his ankle, the cheese falling to the floor. He looked down to see the largest sewer rat making off into the blackness with the cheese. It had bitten him!

"You'll be sorry!" Viper roared, hopping around on one foot, about to go after the rat. Suddenly, a light came on in the dark dungeons. Viper whirled around.

"Mr Virus! Really, you ought to know better!"

Donna, his new PR woman, stood there, looking down her rather long nose disapprovingly. Viper glared at her. He intensely disliked Donna. It appeared that she intensely disliked him too. In other words, they made a great team.

"How many times have I told you not to play with those rats? People do not like rats! And they will not like *you* if they find out that rats are your best friends!"

Viper sulked. He was fed up taking orders from Donna. Still, he needed her if he was going to become world dictator. He'd hired her after hearing about the great job she did on Santa Claus. Santa had always been a lovely, generous old man, but he'd had a filthy beard down as far as his ankles and a liking for whole cloves of garlic. Donna had taken him in hand and now, Santa had never been so popular. Viper hoped that soon, he would be even more popular.

"Upstairs now!" Donna commanded, and Viper slunk past her like a bold child. Donna sighed heavily. It had been a drastic mistake, she decided, taking Viper on as a client.

He was totally unmanageable, and extremely rude into the bargain. But, unfortunately, she had allowed her natural greed to overcome her distaste. After all, a girl's got to make a living.

But it wouldn't do her career any good if Viper turned out to be a publicity disaster. And the way things were going, she wasn't at all confident. She decided that she'd have to work very hard indeed to make Viper in any way consumer-friendly.

With new resolve, she set off up the stairs after Viper, pushing to the back of her mind her unease about his subliminal messages and his plans for the world's children. In her job, she couldn't afford such luxuries as morals.

"This way," Viper spat over his shoulder, hoping that maybe she'd gotten lost in the maze of dark corridors and tunnels.

Viper Virus lives underground, in a bunker that he discovered years and years ago. He moved in and quickly made it his own, building great sprawling dungeons and dozens of airless rooms that many people had gone into and never come out of again. He contemplated locking Donna into one of those rooms and throwing away the key. She wouldn't be the first.

"That'd be nice," he cackled to himself.

"What?" Donna snapped. Viper limped faster, ignoring the pain in his ankle. Anything to get away from the odious woman.

Viper found a surprise waiting for him upstairs.

"Ah Viper! Good to see you, Boss! You're looking very well indeed!"

Jason Ratz bowed and scraped in front of Viper.

Viper brushed him aside with a bat wing and limped on.

"Did you get it?"

Ratz looked confused. "What, Boss?"

"The disk, you idiot!"

Ratz sweated profusely as he dug deep into the pockets of his filthy raincoat.

"Sure, Boss. I got it here. No trouble. Whatever Viper wants, Viper gets. Isn't that right, Boss?"

"Shut up, you fool, and hand it over." Viper was in no mood for Ratz right now. He considered Ratz one of his foot soldiers – someone who would do all the dirty work and take all the risks and then could be dispensed with very easily once there was no more use for him.

Still, it wouldn't do to be too nasty to Ratz – not while he still needed him.

"Good work, Ratz, my boy," he said, managing a smile and displaying several rotting teeth.

"And I lost Mike Rofone!" Ratz boasted.

"No," said Viper with a secret smile. "*I* lost Mike Rofone."

"Huh?" Jason was confused.

"Oh, never mind," Viper said. He wouldn't bother telling Ratz that he'd come across Mike Rofone on the kids' chatlines. And with any luck, Mike was somewhere in Alaska right now, courtesy of Viper.

"The disk," he prompted rudely.

Ratz reverently produced it. Viper turned it over and over in his hands, enthralled. It was a completely innocent-looking computer disk, but only Viper knew what dreadful messages were on it. Here, on this disk, lay his future.

"Make a copy of this later," he instructed Ratz. "And don't forget!"

"Uh, I won't, Boss, I won't."

"Oh, and how is my old buddy Blackrattler?"

Blackrattler, a subliminal messages expert, had secretly made the disk for Viper on the condition that Viper spring him from prison.

"He said that he's waiting for you to come and free him," Ratz reported.

Fat chance, Viper thought. He had gotten what he wanted from Blackrattler and now he could rot.

"Um, Boss?" Ratz now whined.

"What!" Viper snapped.

"I brought the disk to you like you said, yeah?"

"So?"

"So I get to write about it for my newspaper, right? I get an exclusive, huh?"

Viper's eyes narrowed until they were mere slits. "I don't remember anything about an exclusive."

Ratz quaked. "B-but Boss, you promised."

He had, too. He'd promised that if Ratz helped him, Ratz could publish the first account of the takeover of the world by Viper. Such a marvellous scoop would put Ratz right back on top. For too long now, Ratz, through his own laziness and sheer incompetence, had been relegated to the minor league at his newspaper, *The Rattler*. *The Rattler* was a supermarket rag that published mostly silly stories about UFOs and famous people. But lately, Ratz hadn't even been allowed to cover UFOs. He'd been stuck reporting traffic build-ups and roadworks. And he was mad.

"Ah, yes, it's coming back to me now," Viper murmured. "Of course you get your exclusive! Absolutely!"

Viper knew perfectly well that Donna had arranged an exclusive with the largest cable television network in America. Still, it was fun to string Ratz along.

Ratz smiled and grovelled pathetically. "Thanks, Boss."

In a few short days, he'd leave the rest of those stuck-up reporters behind. Reporters like Mike Rofone, who thought they were above everyone else, and who looked down their noses at *The Rattler*. He'd show them all. But especially Mike Rofone.

"Now, to work!" Viper bellowed, triumphantly waving the disk.

"In two seconds flat, every kids' chatline in the world will carry my subliminal messages!" he announced with glee.

"Not quite, Mr Virus."

Viper froze, then turned his awful black eyes onto Donna, who had spoken. Donna was unmoved by his hostility.

"Be sensible," she continued. "It's absolutely stupid to put those messages out worldwide, without finding out first if they actually work. Think of the PR disaster if something goes wrong!"

Viper chewed on his bottom lip, thinking. He hated to admit it, but the woman was right.

"And what did you have in mind?" he asked her, ever so sweetly.

"A test," she answered, just as sweet. "Test the thing out first on one person. And if it works, then we can blitz the Net."

Viper nodded slowly. Then he extended a bat wing and grabbed Jason Ratz by the scruff of the neck.

"Aw, no, Boss, please!" Ratz screamed. There was no way he wanted to be exposed to any kind of subliminal messages, especially if they weren't sure they even worked. He thought fast.

"There's no use trying them on me," he said urgently. "What you need is a kid. A real live kid as a guinea pig. After all, kids are the people you want to reach in the end. Right, Boss?"

Donna tapped a long scarlet fingernail thoughtfully on Ratz's head.

"He's right, Viper."

"A kid? A KID?" Viper roared. "And where on earth are we going to get a kid?"

Ratz grew crafty. "Just so happens, Boss, that I saw a lovely specimen only today. A boy. He was hanging around with Mike Rofone on the Net."

Now Viper smiled too. Ratz knew that the idea appealed to him, especially if Viper thought the boy was a friend of Mike Rofone. Ratz knew of only one person who hated Mike Rofone more than himself, and that was Viper.

"Ratz, dear," Viper murmured, "go and invite this boy to tea."

Where was Mike Rofone?

This question was going around and around Indie's head as he lay in bed. What was Mike up to? Had he caught the villains? Indie hoped so, but, of course, Mike had no way of contacting him – his computer was confiscated. He tried to put the whole thing out of his mind and go to sleep. But he just tossed and turned and then tossed some more. It was no use. He wouldn't get a wink until he found out.

It was very late as he tip-toed quietly past his parents' bedroom in the hall. He stopped for a moment, wondering where his father might have hidden his computer. Downstairs, he guessed.

And, of course, there was his computer, stacked neatly in the cupboard beside the television. Parents, he thought – no imagination.

He turned it on quickly and got on the Net, then looked for a chatline.

Unbidden, Mr Broadhead's words came back to him.

"No! Sorry, Indie, but it's too dangerous... "

Still, thought Indie, he was only going on the chatlines for a minute, and besides, Mr Broadhead need never know...

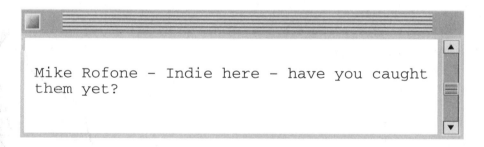

```
Mike Rofone - Indie here - have you caught
them yet?
```

He waited for an answer to his message. No reply. Mike must be on another kids' chatline. But there was no reply on the next one he tried, or the next, or the next.

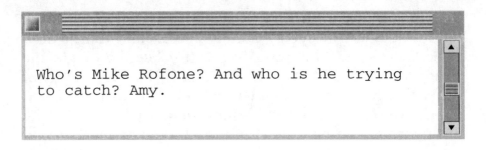

Who's Mike Rofone? And who is he trying
to catch? Amy.

Indie jumped. Someone else was reading his messages. Someone called Amy.

He quickly typed back that he was sorry, but he couldn't tell. He asked her what she was doing up so late.

Because I feel like it.

Wow, thought Indie. If he did everything he felt like doing, his parents would have a fit.

He was about to ask her how she managed to get around her parents, when he suddenly felt a bit odd. He had the weirdest sensation of being pulled towards his computer screen. Another message came up for him.

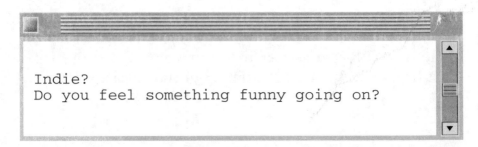

Indie?
Do you feel something funny going on?

Amy obviously felt it too. But there was no time to reply, because now Indie was being sucked nearer and nearer to the screen. Horrified, he grabbed at a chair to try to stop himself, but it was no use. The chair crashed over and he was lifted off his feet.

"Woah!" he howled as the screen came closer and closer and then PLOP! He was inside his computer. With a thud, he landed flat on his back on the same white floor as before.

"This is becoming a bit of a habit," he muttered to himself.

He looked up and met a pair of mean brown eyes. It was Jason Ratz.

CHAPTER 4

Mr Broadhead was stretched out on his leather chair in the middle of the newspaper office, fast asleep and dreaming of all kinds of lovely things.

"Oi! Wake up!"

Mr Broadhead jerked awake with a loud snort and looked around, confused. Who was shouting at him?

"Turn on your computer and let me out!" The voice was coming from his computer.

With a supreme effort, Mr Broadhead got to his feet and staggered to his computer. He turned it on, and slowly, Mike Rofone appeared on his screen. Suddenly Mr Broadhead was wide awake.

"Say, Mike, what happened to *you*?"

Several icicles hung from the fingers of Mike's gloves. Snow clung in great lumps to his shoes, and his eyebrows were white with a thin layer of ice. His mouth had gone a peculiar shade of blue and he was shivering uncontrollably.

He tried to speak.

"I-I-I've just b-b-been stranded in A-A-A–"

"A freezer?" Mr Broadhead offered helpfully.

"No!" Mike tried to go on. "Viper V-V-Virus duped me and sent me to A-A-A-CHOO!"

"Bless you," Mr Broadhead said kindly. "Do you want a tissue?"

"Will you let me finish!" Mike roared. "A-A-Alaska! He sent me to Alaska on a wild goose chase!"

The newspaper office was agog at this latest piece of vileness from Viper. They were thankful that none of *them* had been assigned to the subliminal messages story.

"What happened?" Mr Broadhead asked, concerned now.

Mike was curt. "I found a message on the Net that made

me think that Viper's headquarters were in Alaska. I spent hours and hours trudging through the snow looking for him, and then an avalanche fell on me."

Somebody at the back of the office sniggered. Mike could feel himself burning with embarrassment. He glared around; everybody quickly went back to work.

"Can you get me a hot cola?" he asked Mr Broadhead.

"Hot? Cola?"

"Yes," Mike said irritably. "I'm freezing."

"You know, you drink far too much cola. It's not good for you—"

"Will you get it for me or do I have to go myself?" Mike snapped sourly.

Mr Broadhead looked hurt, then shambled off towards the kitchen area at the back of the office.

Alone, Mike calmed down and immediately felt bad about his short temper. But if there was one thing he hated more than anything, it was to be made a fool of. And Viper Virus had just done that very successfully.

Still, there was no point in taking it out on Mr Broadhead. He'd just have to apologise.

Mike started to feel a little warmer now, and a little better too.

"If Viper thinks I'm beaten, he's another thing coming," he muttered to himself. The Alaska episode had just strengthened his resolve to catch Viper and put him away once and for all.

"Here," said Mr Broadhead holding out a cup of hot cola.

"Thanks," Mike said, managing a smile. "And, hey. I'm sorry. You know, for snapping. I guess I should have smelled a rat sooner."

"Viper's clever," Mr Broadhead said sympathetically.

He certainly is, Mike thought. But he'd come up against clever villains before, and had beaten them.

"Mike?"

Mr Broadhead was looking unusually solemn. "Mike, I think that Viper is just going to keep doing this. Sending us on wild goose chases for his own amusement."

"So? We'll keep going until we catch him," Mike replied.

Mr Broadhead looked pained. "We don't have the resources at this office to keep chasing after Viper forever."

"I'll work for free!" Mike said adamantly.

"That's not the point! The point is that you're my star reporter. I need you here reporting stories for *The Daily Rap*, not spending days and days tracking down Viper Virus!"

Mike was utterly aghast. "But this'll be the biggest scoop this paper has ever had!"

Mr Broadhead sighed heavily. "If we get it. *If.* And the way things are going, I'm not too hopeful."

Mike Rofone jabbed a finger in the air wildly. "But I caught Blackrattler last year! Viper's partner!"

"I know. But you didn't catch Viper," Mr Broadhead said quietly.

So that was it, Mike thought bitterly. Mr Broadhead didn't think he was capable of out-smarting Viper.

But Mr Broadhead had read his mind. "It's not that Mike. I know you'd get him eventually. But what happens if he catches you first, eh? Alaska was only fun for Viper. What if he decides to get serious?"

With a flick of his hand, Mike dismissed concerns about his own safety.

"What about the world's children?" he challenged. "What's Viper going to do to them?"

Mr Broadhead looked unhappy and Mike knew he'd found his mark. But Mr Broadhead again shook his head.

"I'm not responsible for every wrong-doing in this world, Mike. We're a newspaper, not a detective agency. I'll hand over our information to the police."

"But without the disk, we haven't a shred of evidence!"

"Mike!" Mr Broadhead said sharply. "I've made my

decision. You're off the story. You're to cover the series of bank robberies in Idaho, starting tomorrow."

Mr Broadhead shrugged regretfully, then walked off slowly.

Mike Rofone was stunned. He was off the story! Finished! Kaput! Assigned to a series of minor robberies in Idaho, of all places! And meanwhile, Viper Virus ran amuck on the Net, causing havoc and brainwashing kids with nobody to stop him!

It was all too much for Mike, who sneezed violently again. He wiped his sore nose in silent misery.

"No," he said softly to himself. "No way, Viper. Not this time."

He was going after Viper Virus and that was that. He knew he was becoming a little obsessed with Viper, but *somebody* had to stop him, didn't they?

"AAAA-choo!" Painfully, he got to his feet and climbed slowly into Mr Broadhead's computer.

"Where are you going?" Mr Broadhead was watching suspiciously from the back of the office.

"Home. I've got flu," he lied.

Wouldn't do to tell Mr Broadhead that he was going in search of some help to track down Viper. From Indie Johnson, to be precise. If Viper was targeting children, then Mike might be able to learn something by starting with Indie.

He wasn't asleep in his bed. He wasn't getting a late-night snack in the kitchen. He wasn't on his computer. In fact, Indie Johnson wasn't anywhere he was supposed to have been.

Mike Rofone stood in the middle of the Johnsons' living-room, worried. The house was very quiet, with everybody asleep. But where was Indie? What was going on?

He'd just arrived in the Johnsons' house via the Net. Indie's computer was, for some strange reason, sitting beside the television – and it was switched on.

Why was Indie's computer switched on when there was nobody using it?

It was then that Mike noticed the last thing that had been typed onto the screen.

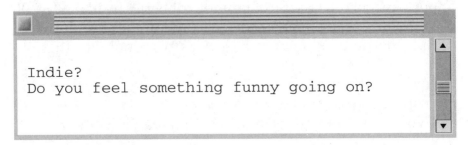

```
Indie?
Do you feel something funny going on?
```

The message was from someone called Amy. And it was on a kids' chatline…

"We told him to stay off the chatlines tonight!" Mike muttered, growing more worried. But what had happened then?

His heart stopped as he saw the next clue. On the floor in front of the computer sat Indie's slippers – minus Indie.

"He's been snatched!" Everything was horribly clear to Mike now. And he had a gut instinct that Viper Virus was behind Indie's mysterious disappearance.

Without wasting another second, he sat himself down in front of Indie's computer. Typing furiously for more than ten minutes, he sent e-mails all over the globe.

Then he sat back and waited. Sure enough, messages started to arrive back within seconds.

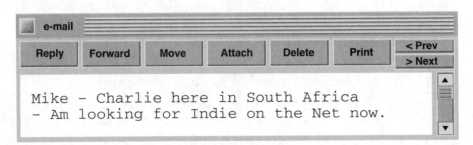

```
Mike - Charlie here in South Africa
- Am looking for Indie on the Net now.
```

Mike grinned. Good old Charlie. Then another message came in.

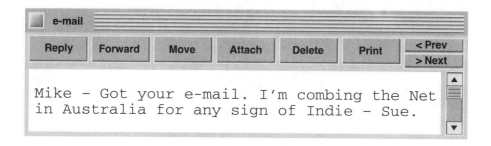

```
e-mail

Reply    Forward    Move    Attach    Delete    Print    < Prev
                                                          > Next

Mike - Got your e-mail. I'm combing the Net
in Australia for any sign of Indie - Sue.
```

Sue was on the ball, too. And more e-mails came in, from Mike's contacts and friends all over the world – India, Sweden, South America, Iran and Morocco, to name but a few. These people were all Internet experts and right now, they were on-line looking for Indie.

All Mike could do was sit and wait.

A horrible scratching noise came out of the darkness.

"Amy?" Indie gulped. "Do you hear that?"

Beside him, he could feel Amy stirring. He couldn't see her, because the dungeons were pitch black, but he knew that she was nearby.

"Yeah. It sounds like rats."

To Indie, Amy sounded very casual indeed, as though rats and dungeons were daily occurrences for her. The scratching noise came again, nearer. Indie quaked. Suddenly, he heard Amy shuffling forward on the floor, towards the noise.

"What are you doing?" he hissed, horrified.

But Amy kept moving forward.

"Now listen here, rats!" she said sharply. "We don't mean you any harm, so we'd be obliged if you'd go off and scratch about somewhere else, okay?"

The scratching noise abruptly stopped. Then Indie could hear tiny feet retreating rapidly, until there was silence.

"How did you do that?" he asked in grudging admiration, annoyed that this Amy girl didn't seem to be frightened of anything. She hadn't been frightened when Jason Ratz had tossed the pair of them into these filthy dungeons. And she hadn't seemed at all ruffled when he'd blown out the candle, leaving them in this awful darkness.

"I just guessed that the rats were probably more scared than we were."

"You mean you're scared?" Indie scoffed.

"No," she said. Then, a pause. "I'm terrified."

"Oh." Indie immediately felt better. So he wasn't the only one.

They huddled together companionably until their shoulders touched. Both were very glad that they weren't alone.

"Listen, Amy. I'm sorry about this. They were only after me."

Amy shrugged. "Well, now there are two of us. We've got a better chance against Viper."

Indie felt even better now. He decided that Amy was okay in his book. He'd already told her all about Mike Rofone and Jason Ratz and how Viper was planning to flood the Net with subliminal messages.

"Have you seen this Viper Virus guy yet?" she whispered now.

"No," Indie answered. But they both knew they'd be meeting him very soon.

Indie shivered. Was it just the cold, or the thought of meeting Viper? He was glad when Amy took off her coat and spread it over them.

"What were you doing on the Net so late?" he asked, trying to take his mind off Viper.

"I can do whatever I want," she replied loftily.

"But don't your parents mind?"

She didn't immediately answer. Indie thought that maybe she didn't hear him. But she had.

"I don't think my parents even notice," she said in a small voice. Then, quickly, she changed the subject. "Hey, Indie, where are you from?"

"Dublin."

"Yeah? I'm from Canada. Toronto."

"I've never been to Canada."

"Tell you what. When we get out of here, I'll invite you over for a holiday. How about that?"

Indie doubted whether he'd be let down to the corner shop, never mind Canada, once his parents discovered he was missing once again.

"Sure," he said, just to keep his spirits up.

There was silence for a long, long time. Hours passed.

"Indie? Are you awake?"

He was.

"I've got a plan. If Viper is planning to put these messages out on the Net, that means he must have a computer here somewhere, right?"

Indie nodded slowly. "Right. So maybe one of us can get to this computer—"

"And e-mail Mike Rofone!" Amy finished.

It was definitely worth a try. In fact, it was the only hope they had.

"Okay," Indie whispered. "We'll try to distract Viper—"

There was an unearthly shriek. "Did I hear my name mentioned?!"

Indie and Amy froze in fright. They heard a match cracking, and next thing, a candle bobbed above them. And in the light of the candle was an awful vision. Viper Virus.

"I see that you've made friends," he said sarcastically. "Aw, ain't that sweet?"

Indie and Amy shrank further back as Viper hovered closer,

looking from one to the other.

"Sooooo," he drawled. "I've got two horrible kiddies instead of one. Still, waste not, want not, eh?" And he cackled manically, setting Indie's teeth on edge. In the meagre light of the candle they could see their surroundings. The dungeons stretched far, far back before the darkness gobbled them up. Filthy water dripped constantly into a huge black puddle on the ground nearby. Cobwebs fell in great blankets from the ceiling.

"We're going to have such FUN together!" Viper twittered.

"You let us go now!" Indie shouted. "You've no right to keep us here!"

Viper's good mood evaporated in a flash. He held the candle close to Indie's face and took a good look.

"So," he said. "Here's one that looks like trouble."

It was the story of Indie's life. He just had the kind of face that looked like trouble. And it wasn't working to his advantage right now.

"Listen, Mr Virus. We won't cause any hassle. Just please let us go and we won't tell a soul."

Viper was amused. "Dream on."

Indie threw a look at Amy. So far, she hadn't said a word. In fact, for all her brashness earlier, she was now cowering against the wall, trying to hide behind her hair. She looked thoroughly scared and defeated. Indie immediately smelled a rat.

"Mr Virus?" She smiled meekly up at him, two cute little dimples coming to her cheeks. He swung the candle towards her. She dropped her eyes shyly.

"I'm feeling a little thirsty. Would you mind awfully if I went over there to that dripping water and had a little sip?"

Her voice managed to sound very frail and broken.

Viper looked her up and down slowly. Then, with a flick of

his bat wing, he dismissed her as a potential source of mischief.

"Make it snappy," he bit, and stood aside to let her pass. Then he turned back to Indie.

"Fancy being a guinea pig?" he taunted.

Indie looked at the floor, determined not to let Viper see how scared he was.

"Mike Rofone will get you," he said quietly. But to his surprise, Viper wasn't annoyed. In fact, he seemed to find this extremely funny.

"Not if I get him first. In Alaska," he giggled hysterically.

Alaska? Indie wondered what Viper was talking about.

Viper eventually managed to get himself under control. "Now, on your feet, boy. And you, girl! Get back here, pronto!"

Only there was no reply from Amy. Viper's eyes grew wild, as he swung the candle high into the air, bathing the dungeons in eerie light. There was no sign of Amy. In a fury, he threw the candle and matches to the ground and howled.

Indie's heart quickened as he heard footsteps far away pounding the floor. Run, Amy, run!

CHAPTER 5

Amy, breathless now, sped through the dungeons, her legs hurting and her lungs about to burst. Up ahead, she could see that the huge corridor split into several smaller tunnels.

She slowed down and veered right. A dead end. She whirled around to the left. Oh no. Another dead end. What now?

"AHHHHH! When I get hold of you, you'll wish you were never born!!!"

The hysterical shriek came from behind her. Viper Virus was closing in fast.

She looked around wildly. And then she saw it. A tiny passage, almost hidden. She took a deep breath and plunged down it.

The passage was so narrow and low that she had to bend her head. This made running even more difficult.

"Come on, Amy! You can do it," she chanted to herself, and ran faster. Her teacher in school didn't write the word "determined" on her school reports for nothing.

A bat screeched to her left. Then, something – or someone – touched her hair. She lunged on, half-stumbling with fright. Surely the passage had to end soon? And it did. Suddenly, she was up against a large door. There were huge red letters painted boldly across the wood.

DO NOT ENTER! DANGER!

"It can't be any more dangerous than out here," she muttered, and gripped the handle. But it wouldn't open. She tugged and pushed and pulled, but the door wouldn't budge.

Growing ever more frantic, she had no choice but to turn back, speeding haphazardly down the tunnel, wondering where she could go next.

She spied another doorway to her left, open this time. She

veered into it, coming to a dead stop, blinking in confusion as she was bathed in blinding light.

"Wow," she breathed in awe, looking around, wide-eyed.

State-of-the-art computers sat on every available space – some blinking with colourful lights, others spitting out sheet after sheet of paper, more still whirring and grinding and humming. It was like some fantastical room straight out of a science fiction movie.

Spoiling the whole effect was Jason Ratz, who sprawled untidily in a chair, scoffing a hot dog. He was supposed to have been copying the subliminal messages disk, but had decided to have a snack first.

Amy rapidly started to retreat. Too late. Ratz had seen her. "What are you doing here?" he said roughly, getting to his feet. She had to think fast. She took a deep breath, filling her lungs.

"Excuse me!" she bellowed, "but what are *you* doing here?"

Ratz froze in shock. He'd never heard such a loud voice coming from such an angelic-looking little girl.

"I'm supposed to be here," he answered meekly.

Amy shuddered in distaste as a huge glob of ketchup fell from Ratz's scrawny moustache onto his coat.

"Yeah?" she spat. "Well I was sent to look for you! We're all waiting on you downstairs and Viper Virus is absolutely FURIOUS with you!"

Ratz dropped his hot dog in fright. "W-what?"

She shrugged casually. "He said he was going to feed you to the rats."

Ratz jumped to his feet, quaking. "I'd better get down there fast. Come on."

Seeing as he was so gullible, she decided to use it to her advantage. She shot a glance towards the computers.

"In a minute. Viper told me to order out for pizza. On the Net."

But now Ratz was suspicious. "Viper only eats meat. Raw meat and maybe a little cheese."

"Oh?" Amy blustered, caught. She'd have to bluff her way out of it. "Well, I'll just have to go down and tell Viper that you said he couldn't have a pizza—"

"No!" Ratz howled, pushing her towards a computer. "You go right ahead."

Casually, she said, "Where will I say it's to be delivered to?"

"Huh? Oh, just tell 'em to leave it at the outskirts of the desert, the usual place. I'll have to leave the bunker to pick it up," he mumbled, already on his way out the door.

The minute he was gone, Amy ran to the nearest computer. As luck would have it, the computer was already on-line and she immediately started to compose an e-mail, trying to remember what clues Ratz had given her...

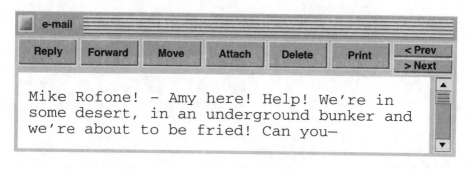

"Soooo. We've found the little monster."

The hairs rose on the back of her neck. She whirled to see Viper suspended high in the doorway, his awful bat wings pumping the air. Then, with a surge, he swooped downwards.

She frantically stabbed at a key on the computer and sent the e-mail, a split second before she was grabbed by the hair on her head and lifted clean out of her chair. "Ouch!" she yelped, dangling in the air.

"Quite the little actress, aren't we?" Viper sneered. "Only down here, you don't get any Oscars."

He dropped her back into her chair.

"And as for YOU!" he roared, as Ratz came crawling into the room, dragging Indie by the shoulder.

"Sorry, Boss, uh, I guess I made a mistake. I thought you wanted a pizza..."

Viper rolled his eyes skywards in utter despair.

"Be quiet, you moron! Why am I surrounded by utter imbeciles?"

Ratz tried to look helpful. "I dunno, Boss, maybe it's because—"

Viper gritted his teeth. "That was a *rhetorical* question, you fool! It wasn't meant to be answered!"

Ratz was now hopelessly confused. "Then why did you ask it, if you didn't expect an answer—"

"Shut up! SHUT UP! SHUT UP!"

Viper was in a black rage now. He hopped around the floor, spitting and gnashing his teeth, his bat wings slapping together dangerously.

Indie, Amy and Ratz shrank away, terrified at this display.

"What's going on here?" a voice calmly asked.

Viper froze in mid-hop. Donna stood with her arms folded, her lips pursed in disapproval.

"Nothing," Viper spat, embarrassed.

"You really should try to control yourself," Donna said curtly. "Those kind of displays are most unattractive. And remember, we *are* trying to make you attractive, however futile that may seem."

Viper slouched away, speechless. Nobody had ever called him unattractive before.

"And as for you two," Donna said, turning cold green eyes on Indie and Amy. "We'll have to do something with you."

Indie was as speechless as Viper when she whipped out a comb and tidied his hair. Amy found her face roughly wiped with a tissue and her socks briskly pulled up.

Now, Donna turned to Ratz. She slowly took in his filthy raincoat and his unshaven face. "I don't think there's any hope for you," she said kindly.

Ratz could feel his face burning. So maybe he was no oil painting, but he wasn't that bad.

"Enough of this image thing!" Viper growled. "Let's get to work."

He produced the disk containing the subliminal messages, and was about to slide it into the nearest computer when Donna sharply rapped his knuckles with her comb.

"Not just yet, Viper."

Now she was busily fixing a camera on a tripod.

Viper was flabbergasted. "What's all this?"

"Publicity shots for the newspapers and television networks," she explained with elaborate patience, as though Viper were rather slow.

"Oh. Right," Viper grudgingly conceded. He rather fancied the idea of being famous.

Indie edged closer to Amy. "Did you manage to send the e-mail?"

"I think so. But I don't know if I gave Mike enough to go on," she whispered back.

"Smile!" Donna commanded, from her position behind the camera.

Nobody smiled except for Viper, who was still dreaming of his future as a star. Bits of cheese and raw meat decorated his rotting molars.

Donna emerged from behind the camera. She pointed wearily at Viper.

"Go and wash your teeth."

"Aaah-aaah-CHOO!"

Mike groaned and blew his nose. He felt even worse than he had yesterday.

The fact that he hadn't gotten any sleep last night didn't

help either. He'd slipped out of Indie's house before dawn, after spending the entire night on the Net searching for him. A fruitless search, too. Not one of his contacts on the Net had come across a single sign of Indie. He seemed to have vanished into thin air.

"And now I've to face Mr Broadhead," he groaned, wiping his nose again.

He would be expecting a full report on the Idaho bank robberies. Needless to say, Mike hadn't spent a minute on the story.

He decided that he'd better come clean straight away.

"I've a confession to make," he announced, as he barged into the newspaper office. Unusually, Mr Broadhead appeared to be actually working. He was hunched in front of Mike's computer.

"Mr Broadhead?" Mike moved closer.

"Get out of the way, quick!" Mr Broadhead rudely pushed Mike away from the computer screen.

Oh, that's lovely, thought Mike. Just lovely.

"I haven't done a single thing about the Idaho robberies!" There. He'd said it. Mr Broadhead would probably have a fit.

"Good," Mr Broadhead mumbled, still glued to the computer screen.

Mike decided that he hadn't heard him.

"In fact, I've been following the Viper Virus case all night!"

This was sure to incense Mr Broadhead. And indeed, he looked up straightaway.

"Excellent! And did you come up with anything?"

Mike was baffled. "What do you mean, did I come up with anything? You put me off the story, remember! AAAH-CHOO!"

"Bless you," Mr Broadhead said. "You really should do something about that cold."

"Stop trying to change the subject!" Mike yelped. "Are you denying that you took the Viper Virus story from me?"

Mr Broadhead managed to look sheepish. "I've changed my mind. But listen, never mind about yesterday. Something has just happened!"

"I know," Mike snapped. "Indie's missing!"

But Mr Broadhead didn't seem surprised. Instead, he pointed to Mike's computer. There, in the middle of the screen, was Amy's frantic message for help.

Mike's heart sank. His worst suspicions were confirmed. Viper Virus had Indie in his clutches, and worse again, he'd obviously kidnapped this Amy girl too.

"This is terrible," Mr Broadhead muttered, shaking his shaggy head.

Mike was quickly reading the message again. "She doesn't say where the bunker is. We haven't a hope of finding them!"

"This is terrible," Mr Broadhead said again.

"There must be hundreds of deserts in the world. We can't possibly search them all," Mike added in despair.

"This is terrible."

"We know it's terrible. The question is, what are we going to do?"

Mr Broadhead slumped back in his leather chair, his eyelids starting to droop. He'd been working flat out since seven this morning and he was bone tired. But judging by the way Mike was pacing, he guessed that forty winks was a long way off.

"A bunker. She mentions that they're in a bunker," Mike said slowly, his eyes lighting up. "What does that say to you?"

Mr Broadhead was confused. "Nothing very much."

"Ordinary people don't go around building bunkers," Mike added, waving his arms dramatically. "I mean, have YOU ever built a bunker?"

Mr Broadhead sat up. "Not that I can remember. Mind you, I built a tree-house once. It was very nice indeed—"

"Later," Mike said, cutting him off.

The penny finally dropped with Mr Broadhead. He sat up in excitement. "Governments generally build bunkers!"

"Exactly!"

But just as quickly, Mr Broadhead slumped back into his seat. "If it's a government bunker, we haven't a hope of finding out where it is. That kind of detail will be on a state computer. Classified information. We don't have access to it."

There was silence for a moment. Then Mike spoke quietly and pointedly. "But that's never stopped you before, has it, Mr Broadhead?"

Mr Broadhead jerked forward as though he'd been stung. "No, Mike!"

"Yes, Mr Broadhead."

"I can't do it!"

"Yes you can."

Mr Broadhead had a little secret that only Mike Rofone knew about. Before he became the esteemed editor of *The Daily Rap*, Mr Broadhead had carved out a very nice living for himself as a computer hacker. That is, breaking computer codes and getting into privileged information. Very shady ground indeed, and he prudently never mentioned his former career. But, of course, Mike Rofone had sussed it out years ago.

"It's unethical! It's totally unethical for a reporter to do something like that!" Mr Broadhead protested strongly.

Mike looked sly. "A reporter? And tell me, when was the last time you actually wrote an article?"

Mr Broadhead blushed. He usually left any hard work – like reporting – up to someone else.

"Well, it's – it's immoral!" he said.

He liked to think that he had high morals. Well, sometimes they slipped, but didn't everyone's occasionally?

"People are in danger here!" Mike urged.

Mr Broadhead made one last stab. "I could go to jail if anyone ever found out!"

"So I'll come and visit you."

Mr Broadhead was defeated and they both knew it. Mike Rofone leaned in, looked serious. "You know I wouldn't ask you to do something like this if there were any other way. I wouldn't ask you to do it just for a scoop. But Indie and Amy are in danger."

With a heavy sigh, Mr Broadhead tugged his swivel chair closer to his computer and prepared to break into highly sensitive government information.

Mike Rofone hung over his shoulder, watching. "And don't worry, Mr Broadhead. Nobody will ever find out."

Miles and miles and miles away, a woman looked up from her desk, puzzled. Her computer was telling her that something or someone was interfering with it. She immediately buzzed her boss.

"Senator? I think we've got a problem."

CHAPTER 6

The snake slithered to a stop.

Black eyes glared, unblinking. Then, the snake opened its mouth and a long red forked tongue darted out, then back in again. Lazily it slithered forward another inch. Mike Rofone gulped, but didn't move a muscle.

"Nice snake. Nice snakey," he murmured, trying to sound friendly.

The snake glared some more. Trembling, Mike slowly extended his can of cola. "Wanna sip?" he offered generously. "Hey, I don't share my cola with just anyone, you know."

The snake was unimpressed.

Mike and the snake had been in a stand-off for about ten minutes now. They'd run into each other by accident, and it hadn't been pleasant for either of them.

"Look," Mike tried to reason with it, "you're from this neck of the woods, right? Well it's all new to me, so how about you give me a break here, huh?"

He was in the middle of the Nevada desert, searching for Viper Virus. Mr Broadhead's forays into the government's central computer had yielded a long list of state-owned bunkers – but only one was located in a desert. He'd also found out that this particular bunker was a nuclear one, designed to protect high-ranking officials should there be a nuclear fall-out. But it had been abandoned now for over ten years, since the end of the Cold War.

Mike had been making great progress in tracking it down until he came up against the snake.

"Hissssss!" With an ominous rattle, the snake slithered forward another inch.

Mike decided that enough was enough. If this snake wasn't

going to be sensible about things, then he'd just have to take matters into his own hands.

Moving very slowly so as not to antagonise the snake, he reached up towards his neck and felt for the ON/OFF switch that all microphones have. He stealthily switched himself to ON.

Then he cleared his throat.

"NOW LISTEN HERE, SNAKE! THIS DESERT AIN'T BIG ENOUGH FOR THE BOTH OF US!"

His amplified voice rolled across the desert, hit the mountains in the distance and echoed back. The sheer volume of it was deafening. The snake jumped clean into the air with fright. It gaped at Mike, shell-shocked. Then it turned tail and escaped as fast as it could into the rocks.

Mike shook his head to clear the buzzing noise in his ears.

"Sometimes, I forget my own strength," he muttered darkly.

Eventually, when he could hear himself think again, he briskly consulted his map.

By his reckoning, he was standing more or less over the bunker. He put on his sunglasses and peered around. He could see rocks and dirty sand and more rocks and some wilted weeds. A miserable cactus or two fought for survival in the heat. But there wasn't any sign of a bunker. Nor of Indie and Amy for that matter.

"Phew, it's hot." He wiped his forehead for the zillionth time. At least the heat seemed to have cleared his cold. He hadn't sneezed in hours. He reached into his pocket for a cooling cola. But there was none left... he'd drunk his last cola!

It was then that Mike Rofone realised he was in serious trouble. It was getting towards midday, the hottest time in the desert. He wouldn't survive an hour without shelter and liquid. He needed to find that bunker and he needed to find it fast.

Viper Virus was scrubbed clean. His hair was newly washed and blow-dried into becoming curls, and his bat wings had just received a good polish.

"Sit still!" Donna ordered, as she aimed a bottle of aftershave at him and sprayed.

"Yuck!" Viper spat in revulsion.

Donna's jaw tightened. She'd just about had enough of Viper Virus and this whole set-up. It had taken her all afternoon just to make him half-way presentable.

"Oh stop being so childish!" she said crisply. "If you're to become world dictator, then you have to look the part. There. Finished."

She held up a mirror for Viper to see. Viper, suddenly bashful, turned slowly and took a peek. The mirror promptly cracked.

"Ahhhh!" Enraged, he grabbed the mirror and proceeded to smash it to pieces. Donna closed her eyes in absolute despair.

Across the dim, dark corridor, in the computer room, Indie and Amy quaked as they heard glass smashing.

"Guess he's in a temper again," Ratz cackled, eyeing them evilly. Ratz had been assigned to stand guard over the pair, while Viper got ready for his first press conference, due to take place just after they'd completed the subliminal messages test on Indie and Amy.

"Get lost," Amy said rudely.

Ratz glared at her, then slouched away to chew at his filthy fingernails.

"Don't make him mad!" Indie hissed.

"Why not? It's not as though he's going to help us, is he?" Amy returned.

It was true. There was nobody to help them. Very shortly, they were going to become Viper's guinea pigs.

"I guess Mike Rofone didn't get our message," she added, defeated.

"Guess not. Or else he didn't have enough to go on." Still, Indie found that hard to believe. He had a gut instinct that Mike Rofone was going to show up and save the day sooner or later.

"How long have we been here?" he asked suddenly.

She shrugged. "I don't know. Best part of a day, I suppose."

Indie groaned. His parents. They were bound to be worried. And once they got over their worry, they were bound to be furious.

But he didn't care. He could handle their fury, if only he got out of here in one piece.

"I just want to go home," he muttered.

"I suppose."

He looked at Amy curiously. "You don't seem too enthusiastic. Your parents will be up the walls with worry."

She considered this. "Maybe. Depends whether my Dad has a big board meeting, or Mum has an important client to see. If they don't, then they might miss me."

Indie was shocked. "Of course they'll miss you!"

She looked unsure. "Well, they might. But we all kind of do our own thing in our house. Everybody's busy with themselves."

He thought that this sounded wonderful. Imagine being able to do his own thing all day every day, with nobody to bother him...

"How about you?" she asked curiously.

"Ha! Fat chance," Indie grumbled. "I have people looking over my shoulder every step I take. I've even been grounded for something I didn't do!"

"You've been grounded?" she said, looking wistful. "It's years since I've been grounded."

"Well you're not missing out on anything!" he answered with spirit.

"I know. But it kind of shows that they take notice of you."

He supposed this was true. But couldn't there be a happy balance? Couldn't he do his own thing for a while, like Amy, and only get grounded when he actually did something wrong?

They were both deep in thought on the subject of being grounded, when Ratz hovered over them again. He made a big show of tucking into a huge bacon sandwich.

Indie's stomach rumbled. He was starving. Their host, Viper, hadn't bothered to offer them breakfast.

"So," Ratz drawled, eyeing Indie meanly. "You're a friend of Mike Rofone?"

"Yes," Indie said defiantly. "And he's worth ten of you!"

"That so?" Ratz smirked. "Well let me tell you something. I'm about to get an exclusive for my newspaper on the subliminal messages. Your friend Mike Rofone will soon be relegated to the typing pool."

He sniggered unpleasantly at the thought of this.

"Aren't you ashamed of yourself?" Amy suddenly asked.

Ratz looked at her furtively. "Whaddya mean?"

"I mean kidnapping us. And helping Viper to use that disk to brainwash other kids!"

Ratz didn't quite meet her eyes. "I've done nothing wrong. None of it was my idea, okay!"

Amy and Indie glared at him disdainfully. "If I were you, I'd just be sick with myself," Indie added casually.

Ratz grew more defensive. "So maybe I'm not mad on Viper's methods, but I can't stop him."

Amy leaned forward suddenly in her chair. "But you could let us go, couldn't you? Come on, I know you're a decent guy underneath all that."

Indie nodded vigorously in agreement. Ratz looked slightly bashful at this unexpected praise of his character.

"We won't tell a sinner," Indie promised, in a loud whisper.

"Naw… I couldn't… Viper'd eat me for breakfast," Ratz quivered.

"Don't be so spineless!" Amy said, losing her temper.

Ratz immediately grew mean again. He lifted the bacon sandwich to his mouth and took another bite, chewing exaggeratedly.

"Hungry?" he sneered.

"RATZ!"

He choked on the sandwich. Viper stood behind him, Donna on his heels.

"Teasing the children, are you?"

Ratz managed a nod, waiting for Viper's anger.

"Good boy, that's what I like to see," Viper smirked, and patted Ratz on the head. Ratz now smirked too.

"Nice hairdo, Viper," Amy offered. Viper's curls bounced about ridiculously.

"Shut up!" Viper hissed, mortified. "You'll be singing a different tune in about ten minutes, young lady, when you've had a brainful of my subliminal messages!"

She shrank back, her bravado gone.

Viper fluttered his wings and flew to the centre of the huge computer room. "Right! Strap the brats in. Oh, and make sure the ropes are *very* tight, won't you?"

Ratz grabbed Amy and started to tie her into a chair. Donna did likewise to Indie. He craned his neck to look up at her.

"Donna?"

Donna gave no indication that she had heard him. She continued to bind him to the chair with a thick rope.

"Donna, do you think you could let my parents know that I'm all right? They'll be really worried."

She hesitated ever so slightly, her conscience nagging at her. She told herself that what Viper did was none of her business, and that she wasn't responsible for these children – she was here to do a job and that was that. But still, she couldn't help a nagging feeling of sympathy for Indie and Amy.

"I'll try," she whispered.

"You'll try what?" Viper snapped, his antennae on red alert.

Donna looked at him haughtily. "I said I'll try to make you look endearing on camera, Mr Virus. I'm always looking for new challenges."

Viper was stung. "You're in danger of being fired!"

"Make my day," she snapped.

Viper backed off fast, afraid of her quick tongue. He took his bad temper out on Ratz instead, who was fumbling with Amy's ropes.

"Hurry up!"

"I'm almost done," Ratz said, injured at this attack.

"What do you want, a medal?" Viper sneered.

"There's no call for that," Ratz muttered under his breath defiantly.

Viper froze in disbelief. Ratz had just answered him back! Between Donna's impertinence and Ratz's back-chat, he was close to having a mutiny on his hands. He decided he'd nip it in the bud, fast.

With a lethal swish of his bat wing, he lifted Ratz in the air. Then, he sank his teeth into the collar of his smelly raincoat, and shook him viciously by the neck as though he were a cat with a mouse.

"Aahhhhh!" Ratz shrieked in pain, as he was tossed from side to side like a rag doll. His face grew red, then purple, then very, very white. At the last moment, Viper flung him onto the ground, where he lay for a moment, unable to move.

Indie, Amy and Donna paled in fright. Viper turned deadly black eyes on Donna.

"Have you any other comments to make, Donna?"

Donna decided that she had been mistaken; she wasn't dealing with a rude, unmanageable maniac – she was dealing with a psychopath.

"No," she said, very quietly.

"Gooooood. Now go and get your video camera. And you, Ratz. Set up your tape recorder for your exclusive interview. You do still want an exclusive for your paper, don't you?"

Ratz, unable to speak, managed a nod. He slunk past Viper and out the door.

"Viper?" Donna's voice was very meek. "I don't want to pressurise you or anything... but I've sold your exclusive interview to the largest cable network in America. You can't give it to Ratz."

Viper smiled nastily. "Of course not. But why not let him do all the work? Let him get the interview on tape, then you just take the tape off him and send it to the cable company. The fool won't suspect a thing until it's too late."

She nodded quickly and slunk out after Ratz.

Now, Viper turned to Indie and Amy, who were frozen in their chairs.

"So hard to find good help these days," he smiled pleasantly. "Now, shall we go to work?"

Amy and Indie exchanged petrified glances as suddenly, a huge computer screen was pushed right up to their faces, so close that they had no choice but to look at it. The screen suddenly came to life as Viper switched it on.

Then he leaned towards them, his foul breath wafting down into their faces.

"Right, kiddies," he crooned, as though he were talking to his pet rats. "I'm going to get my special disk. In about ten minutes you'll be mine."

CHAPTER 7

Mike Rofone was lying under a cactus, trying to shield himself from the desert's midday sun. He was wondering what to do now, and where to go, when he heard a sound. A cough. A cough?

He rolled over stealthily onto his stomach and looked across the sand. His eyes widened in amazement... it couldn't be... it WAS... Jason Ratz!

"Well, whaddya know," he said softly under his breath. But there was something peculiar about Ratz. He was extremely pale, and he was clutching his throat and coughing. The collar of his raincoat was in tatters, as though something or somebody had chewed right through it.

Mike watched as Ratz crawled forward on hands and knees through the desert, gathering speed.

"Question is, where did he suddenly appear from?" Mike asked himself.

He eased forward an inch or two, craning his neck for any evidence of the bunker. But there wasn't a sign of a door, or any kind of entrance to underground. It was as if Ratz had appeared out of nowhere.

"What do YOU think?" Mike said over his shoulder. Coiled up neatly and nestling cosily beside him was the snake. When Mike had dived under the cactus to get away from the heat, he hadn't realised that this was the snake's pad.

The snake, remembering the strength of Mike's voice, had invited him in. The two had become quite chummy.

Now, the snake peered out and shook its head. It hadn't a clue either.

"And the second question is, where is he going?" Mike mused aloud, as Ratz rapidly crawled forward in the sand, looking over his shoulder fearfully, as if afraid for his life.

Ratz knew exactly where he was going – home. He was sorry he'd ever hooked up with that maniac Viper Virus. It was turning out to be one nightmare after another. His near strangling at Viper's hands was the last straw. It was a shame to miss the exclusive interview, but it was just getting too hairy down there.

With any luck, Viper would be too busy with those two brats to miss him for at least an hour. By then, he should be halfway across the desert. Trouble was, he was absolutely roasting. He'd only gone twenty yards, and already he was wilting from the heat. There was nothing for it but to lighten the load.

He stood up, hauled off his raincoat and discarded it.

Next, he emptied his pockets of loose change, gobstoppers and the remains of a pork pie and threw them away. Last, but not least, he hoisted his heavy tape recorder over his head by its strap, and flung it onto the sand. He could always buy a new one.

Yards away, a crafty smile slowly crept across Mike's face as he saw Ratz fling the tape recorder aside. It was the kind every reporter carries around for on-the-spot interviews. And like every tape recorder, it had a microphone attached.

"Wanna do me a favour?" Mike asked the snake. The snake shrugged in agreement. Anything for a quiet life.

Mike leaned in close and whispered in the snake's ear. The snake grinned slyly, before uncoiling itself and slithering off into the sand – right towards Jason Ratz.

"Oh my God," Ratz moaned in terror, as he looked up to see a vicious-looking snake poised in the sand, head raised.

He stumbled to his feet as the snake edged nearer.

"Hisssss!"

He froze as the snake eyeballed him. So scared was he that he failed to notice Mike Rofone slipping up behind him in the desert.

He didn't see him unscrewing the recorder's microphone, pocketing it, then attaching himself instead. Poor Ratz saw nothing but a slow painful death from poison, with nobody to grieve for him but his mother. And she mightn't bother, come to think of it.

He was about to fling himself at the snake's mercy when suddenly it appeared to lose all interest in him. It yawned, stretched, threw him a disdainful look and slithered casually away

"RATZ! What are you doing up there?"

Viper's voice came from deep underground. Ratz's heart did another unpleasant flip. It was too late now. He'd never be able to make a run for it...

"Quit sunbathing and get down here now, you lazy scum! I'm ready for my interview! Do I have to come up and get you?"

Shaking, Ratz gathered up his tape-recorder, coat and the contents of his pockets. He scurried back through the sand towards a large, ugly cactus. He pressed a hidden button under the arm of the cactus, which was, of course, a fake. Suddenly, the cactus, attached to a hidden trapdoor, lifted into the air. Dusty steps led down into the blackness of the bunker.

Ratz scrambled down the steps, cheering up as he looked on the bright side – at least he'd get his scoop for *The Rattler*. With that, he'd finally take the smirk off Mike Rofone's face.

Mike thought he would surely die. Ratz's grubby fingers clutched him tightly around his midriff, cutting off his blood circulation. The fingers didn't smell too good either. Didn't the guy ever wash his hands? Mike shuddered in disgust, and craned his neck to look around him. He could see that they were passing through a dim, eerie corridor. There was a stale, sour smell, and every now and then, beady black eyes would glint from the shadows. Rats!

He felt sorry for Indie and Amy, imprisoned in a place like this. The question was, how could he rescue them?

"RATZ! Will you hurry up! What are you looking for, overtime?"

The unearthly screech ricocheted down the corridor, setting Mike's teeth on edge. He'd heard that voice before. Viper Virus.

"Coming, Boss!" Ratz squealed in terror, and stumbled faster down the corridor.

Mike steeled his nerve and prepared himself for his first meeting in over a year with Viper Virus. He doubted Viper had forgotten him.

"About time, you cretin!" he heard Viper snarl, as they entered a brightly lit room.

Suddenly, Mike was flung onto a table, landing with a sharp thud. The recorder landed beside him.

Very slowly, so as not to draw attention to himself, he sat up and looked around. Immediately, he saw Indie tied tightly into a chair, a filthy handkerchief stuffed into his mouth. Tied to the chair beside him was a girl, who Mike presumed was Amy.

"Hmmmmmhhh!" Indie protested through the handkerchief, as Ratz spun him and Amy around towards a huge computer.

And now, there was Viper Virus. Mike hardly recognised him. He was all dolled up, with a peculiar hairdo and he stank of aftershave. In other circumstances, Mike would have laughed. But this was serious.

"Ready, everybody?" a stern-looking woman asked, poised behind a large camera. Mike hadn't seen her before.

"See this?" Viper was waving a disk in the air, taunting Indie and Amy. Mike froze.

The disk with the subliminal messages! It looked like he'd gotten here just in time.

But what should he do now? Think, Mike, think! It was three to one, with him against Viper, Ratz and the woman. But if he was able to free Indie and Amy, then the odds would be evened. It was the only chance they had.

Slowly, Mike stood and snuck off the table, crept across the floor, and hopped up beside Indie.

"Hmmmm?!" Indie said, his eyes widening in shock and relief.

"Ssshhh! I'm going to untie you and while I'm diverting Viper, I want you to run for your life, okay?"

Indie mutely nodded. Mike looked around in vain for a scissors, or a knife to cut the rope, but there was nothing. After a moment's thought, he quickly pulled out one of his own wires, and broke it in the middle, leaving a sharp, pointed end. He went to work on the rope, sawing it apart bit by bit.

"Donna! Ratz! Position yourselves. Let's rock 'n' roll!" Viper cackled.

Frantically, Mike sawed faster... one more strand... there!

"Remember... run!" he hissed at Indie, before turning to Amy. Her eyes grew round in amazement, but she wisely kept quiet. Mike winked at her and went to work on her rope.

Now Viper was coming towards the computer, the disk in his hand.

Mike could see Ratz advancing from the other side. Suddenly, there was no more time.

"Run Amy! Run Indie! Now!" Mike roared, jumping up and waving his arms to attract attention to himself and away from Indie and Amy.

Viper froze in disbelief. Ratz gaped. Donna, for once, displayed surprise.

"Mike Rofone?" Ratz stammered, as though he couldn't quite believe his eyes.

Viper screamed a warning as suddenly Indie and Amy threw off their ropes and darted past Ratz.

"Catch them, you fool!"

But Ratz was far too out of shape to catch a couple of very fast eleven-year-olds. The pair sped off into the blackness of the corridor, Ratz panting after them. Donna threw down her camera, and set off in pursuit.

Now, only Viper and Mike were left, facing each other over the computer. They watched each other carefully, neither moving a muscle.

"Soooo. We have the pleasure of meeting again," Viper smiled.

"The pleasure's all yours, I can assure you," Mike said quietly.

Viper advanced slowly, his eyes full of menace. Mike, in turn, retreated towards the door.

"You won't do it again, you know," Viper threatened softly. "You won't mess up my plans THIS time."

"Blackrattler's in solitary confinement. Which is where you'll be before I'm through," Mike replied, just as softly.

"Well, we'll just have to see who'll win, won't we?" Viper whispered, just before he lifted his awful bat wings and poised himself for attack, his teeth bared, saliva dripping from his chin.

Mike Rofone did the only sensible thing. He turned and ran.

Mr Broadhead sat meekly in his leather chair, his eyes fixed firmly on the ground. Lying on the desk in front of him was a warrant for his arrest.

"I'm sorry," he muttered. "But there was no other way!"

The two seedy-looking men standing either side of him were unimpressed. With their slip-on shoes and worn tweed jackets, they resembled a pair of down and outs. But their badges, which they'd thrust at Mr Broadhead ten minutes ago, said they were Bud and Chet, undercover agents working for the government.

"Do you realise you've broken the law?" Chet murmured, bored. He hated these mickey-mouse arrests.

"I'd say you'll get ten years," Bud drawled, cleaning his fingernails with the edge of the arrest warrant.

Mr Broadhead looked horrified. "Ten YEARS?"

The man smiled, enjoying Mr Broadhead's shock. "Minimum," he added, and watched as Mr Broadhead grew paler.

"But don't you understand?" Mr Broadhead implored. "I only broke into your computer so that I could save these kids!"

"A likely tale," Chet muttered. "We get nutters trying to break into our computers every month. But most of them come up with a more plausible story."

Mr Broadhead grew redder in the face. He'd explained the situation to them a hundred times, and they just didn't believe him. They'd scoffed at the idea of Viper Virus and his subliminal messages. They obviously thought that Mr Broadhead was stupid or senile, or both.

"What are you going to do now?" he whispered.

"Dunno. What do you think, Bud?"

"Dunno. What do you think, Chet?"

What a pair, thought Mr Broadhead.

"I guess we'd better haul him down to the police station," Chet eventually decided. "On your feet, Grandad."

Mr Broadhead glared at him. Grandad, my eye! Furious, he pulled himself out of his chair. Then, slowly, a thought occurred to him.

"I guess you won't mind if I print this story in my newspaper tomorrow, boys?"

Chet and Bud froze, looking at each other warily.

"Print what?" Bud snapped.

Mr Broadhead shrugged casually. "Oh, just something along the lines that a government-owned building is being secretly used by a renegade to take over the world."

"Huh?" Chet looked uneasy.

With a dramatic wave of his hand, Mr Broadhead continued. "And that instead of doing something about it, you're arresting decent citizens who are trying to stop him?"

"Hang on a second here—"

"I think it'll go down a bomb with the tax-paying public," Mr Broadhead finished defiantly.

Bud started sweating. Chet moved from foot to foot nervously.

"You can't do that."

"Can't I? Freedom of the Press says I can!"

"Nobody will believe you," Bud said dismissively. "Heck, WE don't even believe you!"

"We'll see, won't we?" Mr Broadhead said mildly.

Chet and Bud exchanged stricken glances. Chet unearthed a mobile phone, turned away and mumbled frantically into it.

Mr Broadhead was feeling very superior after turning the tables on this pair. He wouldn't be at all surprised if he got an award for it. A press award, and maybe others. Hell, he might even run for Mayor…

But Chet was now smiling nastily. He put away his mobile phone.

"You ain't gonna print anything," he said triumphantly to Mr Broadhead.

"What?"

"See, I just got orders to shut down your computer system. *The Daily Rap* isn't going to make it to the news stands tomorrow. In fact, I'd be surprised if it ever made it to the stands again."

Mr Broadhead was absolutely shocked. He couldn't believe that the government had actually ordered this. "Who is your superior?" he thundered.

Chet looked a little furtive. "We're undercover. We don't have to tell you anything. I got my orders, okay? Take out the computer chip, Bud!"

Mr Broadhead groaned. Without a chip, his computer was worse than useless.

"Listen," he said urgently. "Mike Rofone is due to contact me on the Net. If you shut me down, I'll have abandoned him and Amy and Indie! They'll have no way of getting out of the bunker!"

Chet looked more unsettled. "I'm only carrying out instructions."

Mr Broadhead grabbed the nearest phone. "I'm calling your superiors to tell them that there are three people in danger!"

Chet took the phone from Mr Broadhead. "I told them. They know."

Mr Broadhead couldn't quite credit this. "They know, but they're going to pull the plug on my computer system anyway?"

Chet looked at his feet. "They don't want any kind of scandal. As far as the world is concerned, there *is* no Mike or Indie or Amy."

Mr Broadhead paled at this. Chet brushed past him, where Bud was waiting, the computer chip safely in his pocket. They left without another word.

Mr Broadhead slumped into his chair, defeated. Sorry Mike, he said to himself. But you're on your own now.

CHAPTER 8

. . . .

An eerie screech cut through the air.

Indie swung around, his heart in his mouth.

"It's only a bat," Amy quivered beside him.

They were huddled together in a tiny, dark room, unsure of where they were, but too terrified to move.

They'd managed to lose Ratz and Donna in the maze of underground tunnels. Exhausted, they'd come across this room and had slipped inside, pulling the door shut behind them.

"Where's Mike? Why doesn't he come to get us?"

"I don't know."

"I'd say he's probably lost. He'll find us soon enough." Indie tried to sound confident.

"Yeah. He'll be here in a minute," Amy added bravely.

Neither wanted to confront the awful possibility that Viper Virus had done something dreadful to Mike. And that it was Viper, not Mike, who would eventually find them.

"Amy? What are you going to do when you get out of here?" Indie asked, trying to take his mind off the terrible waiting.

"I don't know. I think I'd like to be grounded." She was only half-joking.

Indie thought of his own grounded state almost wistfully. "Yeah. It doesn't seem so bad after Viper Virus."

Amy peered around, trying desperately to see in the murky blackness.

"There's a funny smell in here."

Indie sniffed the air. "Yeah. I wonder what this room is used for?"

Now, he concentrated on his surroundings. He realised

that the floor was extremely soft. He tested it with his shoe. No, not soft, but covered with something.

"Straw?" He picked up a handful. But it was too fine for straw. He quickly dropped it, wondering why it felt so odd.

"If only we had a candle or something," Amy whispered. "We might be able to find a way out of here."

Suddenly, Indie grinned to himself in the darkness and fumbled in his pocket. He'd just remembered.

"You know when you escaped from the dungeons? Viper dropped his candle and matches, he was so shocked. I picked the matches up."

"Nice one!" she breathed in approval. "Quick, let me light one so we can look around."

She carefully extracted a match and struck it. Indie's face bobbed eerily in the meagre light. Amy jumped.

"Sorry. It's just that you look a bit scary in this light."

Indie grinned. "So do you. I guess our nerves are gone."

She held the match higher, looking around. The room was tiny, just four black walls, and the door.

"This is weird," Amy said and moved the match closer to the floor.

"Wonder what that stuff is on the ground," Indie muttered. "What? It's..."

"AAAGGHHHH!" Amy screeched.

"OHMIGOD!" Indie roared.

The floor was covered with a thick blanket of hair – long, silky hair, all shades of black, brown, red and blonde, some with ribbons tied uselessly around it. Human hair... but minus the humans.

Tumbling over each other in their haste, they pushed frantically at the door and landed in a heap in the corridor. Then they ran as if the devil himself were behind them.

Mike could hear the pounding feet getting nearer and nearer, and sweat broke out on his forehead. He'd thought he'd

given Viper Virus the slip, but he was obviously wrong…

He looked around quickly for any kind of weapon.

There was nothing, except a piece of wood hanging off the wooden door he was pressed against. It took only two sharp tugs to rip the strip of wood off.

"Right, Viper. Ready when you are," he muttered, as the pounding footsteps were almost upon him. He held the plank of wood so that it protruded out into the corridor at about knee level. It would trip Viper up, and then maybe he'd have a chance.

"Ouch!" someone grunted. In the dim light, Mike could make out a body somersaulting in the air before landing with a thud. A second body followed. Then silence. Mike looked at the two huddled, frozen figures.

"Indie? Amy?"

Two voices answered, in unison, weak with relief. "Mike Rofone!"

They were on their feet then, and hugging him tightly. Embarrassed, he hugged them back.

"Sorry about that, guys. I thought you were Viper."

"We thought *you* were Viper," Indie returned.

They pulled apart, looking at each other. Mike grinned at Amy, who seemed a little shook.

"Hi. I'm Mike Rofone, by the way. We haven't met."

"Hi. I'm Amy." She managed a small smile. "Can you get us out of here, Mike? Indie said you could."

"Hey, no sweat," he said with a swagger, and saw the relief in their faces. He kept to himself his worries about finding the exit to the desert in this dark maze of tunnels. He also didn't voice his suspicion that Viper Virus was upstairs plotting his revenge at this very minute.

"First things first," he said decisively. "We need to find somewhere safe from Ratz and Donna and Viper. Then we'll put our heads together and come up with a plan, eh?"

Indie and Amy nodded in agreement. Mike looked around the corridor, unsure of which way to go. The corridor branched off into at least five narrower tunnels. It seemed impossible to tell which one would be the best to take.

"Any ideas?" he asked.

Amy nodded slowly. "I think there might be somewhere we can hide."

Then, the entire bunker started to shake in rapid bursts. It was as if some large giant were pounding about upstairs. Dust, plaster and paint started to fall off the walls under the impact.

"Viper," Mike said, trying to keep the alarm out of his voice. "I think it's time to split, huh?"

"Follow me." Amy turned and set off down the corridor, Indie and Mike running rapidly behind.

Amy had to think hard, to concentrate totally, in order to remember the path she'd taken earlier. The problem was, all the tunnels and corridors looked exactly the same...

"We take a right here, I think," she called back to Indie and Mike, hoping that she wasn't totally lost. "And now a left. And we should come to a dead end on either side."

The bunker now shook ferociously and with more frequency. It sounded like Viper was searching the rooms one by one.

"Okay. I think we're... oh no!"

She stopped dead. Indie and Mike crashed into her from behind. Right in front of her stood Donna, who'd appeared silently from a dark passage. The game was up!

But strangely, Donna didn't roar for Viper, or scream for Ratz. She took in their frightened states, and then looked to the ceiling, which was reverberating with Viper's steps. Slowly, she moved aside, motioning for them to go on.

"I never saw you, okay?" she muttered.

Amy smiled her thanks, and scurried past, followed by

Indie and Mike. Indie briefly stopped.

"Do you want to come with us?"

Donna looked tempted, but then shook her head. "I'd better not. Now go!"

She watched as they ran on past her. If Viper found out what she'd done, she didn't dare to think of the consequences...

Why, she wondered, was she jeopardising her own safety for that of a couple of kids and a kooky microphone? Was she getting soft in her old age? Good grief, next thing she'd be adopting stray puppies and helping old ladies cross the road. Alarmed at this prospect, she bent her head and hurried on. Turning a corner, she walked slap bang into Viper Virus.

"Any sign?" he growled, his face contorted with rage.

"No," she said curtly.

"Are you sure?" He was suspicious now. "They must be down here. I've searched everywhere else."

Donna drew herself to her full height, which was considerable. "Well then you haven't searched hard enough, have you? And might I remind you, Mr Virus, that I'm billing you per hour. All this time wasting is going to cost you a bundle, buster!"

She sailed past him, her nose high in the air. Viper grumbled and spat under his breath, before meekly following her.

"You're a very hard woman, Donna," he accused.

"I am, amn't I?" she said, thrilled that she wasn't going soft after all.

On the floor beneath Viper and Donna, Amy had finally found the secret door she was looking for. The sign on the door was luminous in the dim light. DO NOT ENTER! DANGER!

Mike was immediately wary. "What's in there?" he asked Amy.

She shrugged. "I don't know. But they won't think that we'll hide somewhere that's supposed to be dangerous."

Mike was still uneasy. "Well, maybe it *is* dangerous in there. Maybe we should look for somewhere else—"

He froze mid-sentence at a loud thud close behind. Viper Virus was closing in fast.

"Looks like we have no choice," he said urgently.

Amy stepped forward and started to tug and pull furiously on the locked door, to no avail.

Mike Rofone stepped forward gallantly. "Allow me."

Expertly, he plucked another wire from his stomach. In two seconds flat, he'd picked the lock.

"Where did you learn to do that?" Amy asked in awe.

"Ask no questions and you'll hear no lies," Mike said mysteriously.

He ushered the pair in before him, then closed the door and locked it quickly from the inside, using the wire again.

"There. Safe."

At last, all three could take a deep breath and relax. Mike sank down on to the floor in relief. Indie and Amy sat either side of him.

"I knew you'd come," Indie said.

"I almost didn't," Mike replied, thinking of the desert and the snake. "Are you two okay? Viper didn't do anything to you yet?"

"Well, not much, unless you count being locked up and deprived of sleep and food and water," Amy grumbled.

Mike thought longingly of a cola. A tall glass of yummy frosty cola, with three ice cubes and maybe a straw or two... His mouth watered. With difficulty, he dragged his mind back to the matter at hand.

"We've got to outsmart Viper," he reasoned.

"He won't let us out of here without a fight," Indie muttered.

Mike Rofone's mouth twisted with determination. If it was a fight Viper was looking for, then he'd give him one. His mind travelled back to his last encounter with Viper, who was then in cahoots with Blackrattler to destroy the Net. Mike had got the upper hand eventually, because he'd fought Viper on the Net, his own territory. But he wasn't so sure how he'd fare against Viper on his turf, the bunker. So far, he'd just about managed to elude him, never mind put him out of action.

Absentmindedly, he fingered two tiny holes at the back of his neck. Bitemarks, courtesy of Viper, just after Mike had caught Blackrattler and come back for him. Mike didn't want to add another set of his teeth marks to his person *this* time.

"Mike? How much longer before you get us out of here?" Amy asked, in a tired voice.

"All we've got to do is get to those computers," he answered reassuringly. "Mr Broadhead is on red alert to whisk us back to the newspaper office. We just need to get on the Net, that's all."

He tried to sound confident. The big question was, how were they going to get undetected to the computer room?

"We'll be okay," he finished. There was no reply. He looked from Indie to Amy. Both were fast asleep, dead to the world.

"Poor kids. Wouldn't blame them." He carefully eased himself out from between them and stood up.

He decided to have a mooch around, see if he could find any kind of escape route. He remembered the sign on the door in. DO NOT ENTER! DANGER! What could that mean?

He flicked a switch and the light came on. And immediately he saw what the sign meant.

He gave a low whistle under his breath, his eyes scanning the huge shining weapons mounted all around the massive room. He'd only seen these kind of things in photographs before, but he recognised them instantly – they were nuclear warheads. Viper Virus had turned this room into his personal arms depot.

He moved tentatively to the nearest missile, which was mounted on wheels, all ready to be loaded onto a plane and then dropped on unsuspecting people. Mike had seen photographs of the destruction they could cause.

Afraid to touch it, or go too close, Mike could see that the missile was dated and old-fashioned. But still effective enough to blow an entire country off the face of the earth.

This was a million times worse than he had thought. Viper's plans to take over the children of the world was obviously just a first step to something much more sinister and deadly.

And he, Indie and Amy were in the thick of it.

He whirled at a tap on the door. A polite, tentative tap, not loud enough to wake Indie and Amy.

They'd been discovered!

"Who is it?" he whispered through the door, alarmed.

"Ratz," came the muffled reply. "Open up!"

Ratz? "How did you know we were here?" Mike demanded.

"Uh, I guessed,"

"You *guessed*?" Mike was incredulous.

"Yeah," Ratz insisted. "Viper doesn't know. He's given up the search and gone to bed with his pet rats." There was a pause before he politely said, "I've brought you some refreshments."

"Get lost, Ratz."

Again, the voice came from behind the door. "Listen, Mike. We're both reporters here, right? Kind of brothers, yeah?"

"Brothers, my eye," Mike snorted. He'd rather have a

pirhana as a brother than the likes of Ratz.

"No, hear me out. I've kind of had enough of this. Viper's lost it, I mean, really lost it. I want you to take me with you when you escape, right?"

Mike Rofone was silent, mulling this over. He didn't believe Ratz for a second.

"Sorry, Ratz, pull the other one."

Silence from outside. Then Ratz, in a small defeated voice said, "Okay, okay. Wouldn't blame you. I'd better get back upstairs. I'll leave this stuff outside the door. You can take it or leave it, I don't care."

Mike pressed an ear to the door and heard retreating footsteps, then silence. He waited like this for almost fifteen minutes, but there wasn't another sound.

Hmmm, he thought. Refreshments. He sure was thirsty. He knew he was dangerously dehydrated after the desert sun and if he didn't get some liquid soon, he was finished.

Quickly, he hauled open the door, grabbed the tray which was sitting on the ground outside and slammed the door again. No danger.

"Indie? Amy? Wake up."

The two came awake slowly, looking disorientated and confused. Mike placed the tray in front of them with a flourish.

"Food, glorious food! You gotta eat, keep your strength up."

And the three fell ravenously on the cartons of fast food, which were accompanied by three tall glasses of the most delicious cola Mike Rofone had ever tasted. None of them heard a muffled whirring noise over the door, where a hidden surveillance camera discreetly changed direction, recording their every move.

CHAPTER 9

"La LAAA, la di laaa, doo di doo di DAAA!" Viper sang shrilly, totally out of tune but enjoying the sound of his own voice anyway.

He was sitting in the bath, up to his neck in soapy water. This was highly unusual for him.

Normally, he only took a bath on Friday 13th, but today was different. Today was special, and he wanted to be squeaky clean.

His seven pet rats perched around the taps, looking down at him with their beady, suspicious eyes.

"Fancy a swim, my darlings?" he teased, splashing water at them.

The rats vehemently shook their heads. No way. They wouldn't put it past Viper to drown them just for fun.

He scooped up a handful of bubbles and playfully dabbed the nose of the nearest rat. The rat squealed in annoyance and tried to bite him.

Normally, Viper would have hit the roof at such behaviour, but this morning nothing could dampen his mood.

"La LAAAAA!" he sang lustily again, and the rats cringed, covering their ears with their paws. It would be a help if he actually knew the words to the song.

"If you're very, very good, my pets," Viper now said, splashing his feet in childish enjoyment, "I'll let you be in the publicity photo with me."

As if the rats could care less. Their only concern in life was where their next meal was coming from.

"Ah well, bathtime over," he sighed. "Work to be done, to be done, to be done!"

The rats hated it when Viper was in a good mood. He got

all silly and frivolous and you never knew where you stood with him.

Now, Viper was carefully towelling himself dry. The rats hungrily eyed his pink, naked toes, all shrivelled from the bath water. They'd make a darned tasty meal.

Viper reached into the cabinet over the sink, and extracted a huge lump of mouldy cheese. He never gave the rats fresh cheese, always keeping it until it was rotten. He figured it kept them on their toes.

Now the rats eyed the cheese and settled down wearily for the tedious game that Viper always played, mercilessly teasing them and then usually not giving them the cheese at all.

But he quickly broke the cheese into seven uneven hunks, and without further ado, threw these directly to the rats. The rats were stunned. This had never happened in living memory. They held back, suspecting some macabre joke yet to come.

"Today is a special day, my pretties," Viper crooned. "Go on! Eat up!"

The rats needed no further invitation. They grabbed the cheese and dashed out the door, unable to believe their luck.

Viper hummed softly as he checked his appearance in the mirror. He wanted to look just right. After all, this day belonged to him. From now on, people would look at him reverently, they would bow before him, they would call him dictator. Or maybe King? Viper mused on this for a moment. He rather fancied King. It had a better ring to it than "Dictator". King Viper it would be.

Ratz met him at the door to the computer room.

"Everything ready?" Viper asked regally.

"All set, Boss. It worked a dream, your plan," Ratz grovelled.

Viper looked down his nose at Ratz. "From now on, you will address me as King. Not 'Boss'. Got that?"

"Huh? Yeah, sure, Boss. I got it—"

"King!"

"Huh? I mean King. Your Majesty," Ratz hastily amended.

Viper sailed past him into the computer room. The sight that greeted him pleased him very much.

Tied up in two chairs were Indie and Amy, large dirty handkerchiefs stuffed into their mouths as before. Their eyes were still puffy from sleep and they looked confused and disorientated.

"Sooooo," Viper drawled. "We meet again. You didn't really think you'd fool Viper Virus, did you?"

Amy and Indie were, naturally, speechless.

Viper smirked. "Bad luck on your part to have chosen that particular room to hide in."

Amy and Indie looked at him, bewildered. Viper smirked some more. "It's the only one in the entire bunker with a surveillance camera."

He really enjoyed the look of defeat in their eyes.

"I hope you enjoyed the refreshments I had Ratz bring down to you last night?" he enquired politely. "I hope that the large amounts of sedatives I slipped into it didn't spoil the taste?"

He cackled at his own wit. He could see they didn't fully understand. They were obviously confused about last night's events. He couldn't resist elaborating.

"Ratz found you all fast asleep – why, you didn't even finish your burgers. He then dragged you two down here and em, disposed of Mike Rofone."

He could see the alarm in their faces. He smiled.

"You won't be seeing him again. La LAAAAA!"

He accompanied his crude humming with a little victory dance for their benefit. Then with a flourish, he produced a pair of huge shiny scissors and waved them in the air. Amy and Indie exchanged terrified glances. What was Viper planning to do?

"Such lovely hair!" he sighed, tweaking a lock of Amy's hair. She shrank away from his touch.

He smiled at her. "Shame you won't have it for much longer."

Now Indie struggled desperately against the ropes which bound him as Viper came towards him with the scissors.

"Short, but good texture," he decided as he ran a bat wing over Indie's hair. Indie cringed under his damp, odious touch.

"You see, I'm a collector of hair," Viper explained nicely. "Black, blonde, red, brown – I love all kinds. I like to tie it in ribbons and stroke it. Sooo soothing."

Indie shot a quick look at Amy. So now they understood the contents of that small room they'd discovered, with its grisly carpet of hair.

"It's amazing how attached some people get to their hair," Viper mused. "Why, I have to torture some of them horribly before they give it up."

Amy and Indie looked even more terrified.

"Silly of them, really," Viper continued softly. "It's not as if they need their hair where they are now."

Indie and Amy's eyes bulged as this sank in. Then Viper smiled cheerfully and moved in behind Amy, lifting the hair off the back of her neck and placing it along the razor-sharp cutting edge of the scissors. Amy tried to scream but only managed a strangled yelp through the handkerchief in her mouth. Viper hummed busily to himself as he prepared to snip her hair off at its roots.

"Oh for heaven's sake!" Donna snapped, as she entered the room and saw his shenanigans. "Can't you leave those two children alone for two seconds?"

Viper jumped guiltily and tried to hide the scissors behind his back, but Donna was too quick for him.

"What, Mr Virus, do you think you are doing?" she asked icily.

Viper scowled and looked at his feet. "Just gathering a little memento, that's all."

Donna's eyes rolled in utter frustration. "And how do you think those children are going to look on world television with no hair? What kind of advertisement is that for your reign as dictator?"

She held out her hand for the scissors. Viper, sulkily, handed them over. He had to admit that, once again, the dratted woman was right. He'd just have to miss out on the locks of hair this time. It was a shame, this pair had such nice hair; soft and fine. And the floor of his hair room could do with a fresh layer. It was getting a little hard to sleep on. Viper spent the night in this room at least once a week, cosily wrapped in ribboned hair. He always slept like a baby.

"Now just leave those poor kids alone," Donna muttered under her breath, throwing a quick look at Indie and Amy.

Viper's eyebrows jumped up. "Developing a soft spot for them?"

"Nonsense," she said defensively. "I just want to get this test over with, all right?" She started to set up a video camera.

"Fine by me," Viper said, mimicking her voice. "RATZ! Turn on that computer."

Ratz quickly pushed a huge computer forward, so that it almost touched Indie and Amy's noses. Then he turned it on. Donna crouched beside him with the video camera, all set to record every historic moment of Viper's first experiment.

Viper, taking centre stage, slid the disk containing the subliminal messages into the disk drive. He took one last look at Indie and Amy's terrified faces, and smiled evilly.

"It's show time."

Mike Rofone hung from the ceiling by a thick chain tied around his middle. He was suspended in such a way that his feet just barely reached a table that had been placed beneath him and he was forced to stand on tip-toe. The whole thing was cleverly designed to cause the maximum pain possible, and it worked. He wanted to groan in agony, but wouldn't let himself. He was still a little groggy from what he now guessed were the sedatives in the "refreshments" Ratz had brought down.

"I should have been more careful... I should have guessed!" he chided himself. Still, there was no point in recriminations now. He needed to concentrate on getting out of here.

But it's difficult to think when your leg muscles are screaming in pain and your body feels like it's having the life squeezed out of it.

Mike closed his eyes tight and tried to think of something – anything – else.

When he opened them again, Ratz was there, grinning at him.

"Still hanging around," Ratz sniggered, delighted at his little joke.

"Ratz... you scum... you lied last night about wanting to escape from Viper... you tricked us..." Mike panted.

"No kidding," Ratz smiled. "How does it feel to be on the receiving end of trickery, Mike? You probably feel just as stupid as I felt, when I found you'd used me to sneak your way into this bunker yesterday."

Mike wanted to respond, but was afraid he was going to groan again. He bit his tongue hard. He would not show Ratz how bad he felt.

"Did you know that Viper has stocked up on nuclear warheads?" he managed.

Ratz's eyes slid away to the floor. "I don't ask Viper his business, okay? I got nothing to do with warheads."

"But you *know* about them, don't you? Mike said in disgust. "What's he planning to do, Ratz? Blow up the entire world?"

Ratz hesitated, but couldn't resist the temptation to show off what he knew. "He's targeted the world's power centres – Washington, London, Moscow, Tokyo and Sydney – and he's going to destroy them!"

Mike was horrified. "He's going to drop nuclear bombs on them?"

Ratz nodded. "In one foul swoop, global communications will be destroyed and that's when Viper will step in and take over."

Mike's mind was racing. "But he'll have infected everything with radiation! There'll be no food, no water, nothing! Even Viper can't survive that!"

Ratz shrugged. "That's where the kids come in."

"What?!" Mike said.

Ratz explained. "When the world's children are brainwashed, Viper will send out the message for them to get out of the cities and to store up food and water and to take over communications centres. They're going to create power bases all over the world where Viper can rule from after he drops the bombs."

Mike was reeling. What Ratz had described amounted to nothing less than a holocaust. How could he hope to stop this terrible plan before it was too late?

"And you're helping him!" he spat in disgust at Ratz.

Ratz's spine stiffened. He quickly changed the subject. "Got some bad news for you, Mike."

"Shove off, Ratz." He didn't want to hear any more bad news.

"You seen a newspaper today?" Ratz asked suddenly.

Mike gritted his teeth. "How would I have seen a paper, you clown, when I'm tied up here?"

Ratz ignored this abuse. "I thought not. So I brought one for you."

He took a battered copy of his own paper, *The Rattler*, from his pocket.

"Ha! The RATTLER? You call THAT a newspaper?" Mike scoffed.

Ratz glared. "Call it what you like. It's the only one on the market now."

Mike stiffened. What was Ratz on about?

"You see, Mike, it's all worked out rather well. I'll bet you were gonna use Mr Broadhead and the Net to get out of here. Well, he's not gonna help you. And you're out of a job."

Mike decided that Ratz was only trying to taunt him. As if Mr Broadhead would abandon them! And as if *The Rattler* could possibly hope to push *The Daily Rap* off the news-stands! The entire idea was ridiculous.

But Ratz, like a magician, suddenly spread the newspaper and held it up so that Mike could see the front page – and the three inch headline.

THE DAILY RAP MYSTERIOUSLY SHUT DOWN!
WEB SITE DISAPPEARS OFF NET!

Mike was stunned. *The Daily Rap*, shut down? By whom? And why hadn't Mr Broadhead done something to stop it?

Then a worse thought hit him. If *The Daily Rap* was no longer on the Net, then he and Indie and Amy had no way of getting out of here! They were stranded!

Ratz watched with satisfaction the varying degrees of horror crossing Mike's face. He decided it was time for the final blow.

"Oh. And another thing," he said, digging his tape recorder from his pocket. "I just got an exclusive on the whole subliminal messages story for *The Rattler*. It hits the stands tomorrow, with my picture and by-line. Sorry, Mike, but you're history."

Mike carefully kept a blank face. Ratz was a little peeved that he was taking it so well. He'd have liked it if he had

shouted and screamed. It kind of spoiled his victory.

"What's Viper going to do with me now?" Mike asked, as if he couldn't care less. He refused to let Ratz see how awful the news was.

"Dunno. He said to keep you chained up down here until he's finished with the brats upstairs. Then, I'm sure he'll think of something."

Ratz still loitered, even though there was no reason to. He was determined to squeeze every second of pleasure from his triumph – even if Mike wasn't responding exactly as he'd hoped.

"Well, congratulations, Ratz. You're now the number one reporter in the world."

Ratz smiled widely. Mike continued, his voice laden with cynicism, "Shame you couldn't have gotten it by honest means."

Ratz scowled. This wasn't fair! Mike Rofone was taking all the good out of it!

To make himself feel better, he grabbed the chains and yanked Mike a little higher, waiting for his squeal of pain. But instead, Mike yawned elaborately. Livid, Ratz stormed from the room.

Mike hung there, wondering what was going to happen now, and powerless to do anything about it.

Indie's eyes felt as heavy as lead, but he tried not to let it show. He wasn't reading the kids' chatline on the screen in front of him at all, knowing that the subliminal messages were hidden somewhere in the blinking text.

Instead, he focused firmly on the words LIVE CHAT at the top of the screen. It was very tempting to have a quick peek down, even though he knew the messages weren't visible to the naked eye. But so far, he had resisted the temptation, and so far, Viper hadn't caught on to his scam.

"Amy?" he hissed out of the corner of his mouth. "Amy?

Don't read the chatline! Focus on something else!"

But Amy didn't reply.

He went back to staring at the words LIVE CHAT, his eyes growing more and more tired. It had to be over soon... He let his thoughts drift to Mike Rofone. He wondered where he was and whether he was okay.

He didn't want to think too hard about Viper's words that Mike was gone forever... Now his eyes almost closed, he was so tired...

"Enough!" he heard Viper screech, and suddenly, the computer in front of him went dead. At last.

Now, Ratz was before him, roughly untying the ropes that bound him.

"Ouch! That hurt!"

"So sorry," Ratz smirked, and undid the ropes even more roughly.

Indie wanted to kick him, but his mother had told him not to kick people, even rotten people like Ratz. Indie decided he might have a word with his mother about that. If he ever saw her again, that was.

In a few moments Amy was free as well. Indie was relieved that she looked fine.

"You okay?" he whispered. She nodded.

"So, kiddies," Viper smiled from across the room. "Did you enjoy that?"

Indie could see that Viper was watching them very carefully, trying to figure out whether they were brainwashed or not. It was important that Indie convince him that he was under his power.

"Very much, Mr Virus," he answered politely.

"Oh yes, it was great," Amy added, and Indie was glad to see that she, too, was playing along.

"Goooooddd" Viper murmured, stroking his chin with a bat wing. "Still, we won't know how much you enjoyed it until we test you, will we, Ratz?"

"Absolutely, Boss. I mean King. You're dead right there."

"I hate people who agree with everything I say."

Ratz looked confused. "Uh, in that case, no, you're wrong, King."

"WHAT?" screamed Viper. "You're telling me I'm wrong?"

Poor Ratz cowered.

"Shut up and get out of my way," Viper fumed. "Donna! Get your video camera over here. I want to get the tests on tape."

Donna set up her video recorder as Viper glided slowly to a cracked, filthy mirror hanging on the wall. He preened, watching his reflection.

"Mirror, mirror, on the wall, who is the fairest of them all?" he asked softly, before looking to Indie and Amy for the answer.

Indie wanted to snigger – Viper was the most hideous creature on the face of the earth. He winked across at Amy. But she didn't wink back.

"You are, Viper," she answered meekly, looking at Viper with an expression very close to... adoration? No, this couldn't be right, Indie thought with alarm.

"Eh, you're gorgeous, Viper," he quickly added, aware that Viper was now looking at him.

"Hmmmmm," Viper said, not yet totally convinced. "Test number two coming up. I told a little white lie earlier when I said that Mike Rofone was gone forever."

Indie felt relief washing over him. So Mike was all right! But then his heart sank into his shoes at Viper's next words.

"I decided to leave it up to you two to dispose of him. And if you're really good, I'll let you torture him first."

Indie was completely shocked. Viper knelt down between them, looking from one to the other. His voice dropped to a soothing whisper.

"I want you to take him out into the desert and tie him to a cactus. The wild dogs and the snakes and lizards will soon finish him off – that is, of course, if the heat doesn't first. Go, my pets! Go, my pretties!"

To Indie's horror, Amy set off for the door, moving like a robot, a murderous look imprinted on her face.

CHAPTER 10

The newspaper offices of *The Daily Rap* were empty and deserted. Computers were shut down, desks were cleared and the telephones were silent.

Mr Broadhead sat in his leather chair, thinking that he'd never heard the office so quiet, not in all the twenty-five years he'd been editor here.

Yesterday evening, he'd told the staff not to bother coming in today. There was no point, as their computer system had been sabotaged.

"And by the government, of all people," Mr Broadhead said to himself through gritted teeth.

Unusually for him, he hadn't slept a wink last night. Mike Rofone and Indie and Amy had been uppermost in his thoughts. He was imagining their faces when they'd discovered that he, Mr Broadhead, had apparently abandoned them to Viper's tender mercies. Now, he pushed the disturbing image to the back of his mind. He had to concentrate on getting them out of that bunker.

"I've got to get this newspaper back on the Net!" he vowed under his breath. It was the only chance they had of escaping.

An hour passed as Mr Broadhead racked his brains for a way to get his computer chip back from Bud and Chet. But he kept drawing blanks. Another hour passed. More blanks. Eventually, his brain felt as though it would self-combust.

"How, how, how, HOW!" he groaned, thumping his head off the desk like he'd seen in the movies. "Ouch!"

He sat up, nursing the bump on his head, irritable now. And the more he thought of Bud and Chet and their superiors, the more irritated he became.

"In fact, I'm downright FURIOUS!" he informed the

empty newspaper office. "This is the United States of America! It's a free country! Nobody can walk in here and tell me what I can and cannot print, and when I don't agree, they take my computer chip! It's – it's – it's against the law of this land!"

By now, he'd worked himself into a right old state. He stomped around the office, muttering and grumbling under his breath.

A thought struck him, and he froze in mid-step. Bud and Chet and their superiors might have silenced his newspaper, but they hadn't silenced him. He could go over their heads... to someone higher up.

And the more he thought about this, the more he was convinced that the top brass in the country didn't know anything about his computer chip being taken, or about a dissident taking over a government building, or about the threat to the world's children. They simply wouldn't ignore something like that if they knew about it.

"I'll bet that Bud and Chet are trying to do a massive cover-up!" he said triumphantly.

Well, he'd expose the whole thing. He'd take this story right to the very top. And then, he'd demand help to save Indie and Amy and Mike.

His mind made up, he sat down at his desk and plucked up the phone. He dialled quickly.

"Hello? Can I speak to the President?"

Amy moved stiffly down the dark corridor towards the dungeons, her eyes glazed and her face empty of all expression. Indie ran beside her, watching her anxiously.

"Amy? Amy, are you okay?"

"What's wrong?" someone growled behind them. Indie turned to see Ratz bringing up the rear, watching them both suspiciously.

"Nothing," Indie replied innocently. "We were just wondering how long it would take the desert to finish off Mike Rofone."

"Not long, I hope," Amy declared, to Indie's horror.

Ratz looked at them doubtfully. "Good. I was told to keep an eye on you – just in case."

Indie grew more anxious as they reached the dungeons. He had to let Mike Rofone know what was about to happen, so that they could make a dash for it when the opportunity came. The only problem was that they'd have to fight not only Ratz, but also Amy, by the looks of it.

Mike Rofone raised his head with difficulty as the trio entered his cell. His entire body was numb. He was beyond pain.

"Hi, Mike. You're looking a bit pale," Ratz sniggered.

Mike ignored Ratz. He was watching Indie and Amy carefully, wondering what was going on. They were both so solemn and unsmiling...

"Okay, kiddies. Go to work!" Ratz commanded.

Indie gulped and watched as Amy took hold of the chains and started to lower Mike to the table. At last, Mike could feel some function returning to his body, as the blood coursed through his arms and legs.

"Hey, Mike?" Amy said, in a funny, stiff little voice. "We're gonna take you out into the desert and leave you to fry."

Ratz sniggered again. Mike was shocked, but managed not to let it show.

He anxiously searched Indie's face. But Ratz was also watching Indie.

"Yeah," Indie said, trying to sound harsh. "Afraid so, Mike. You're history."

Now, Mike was doubly shocked. Viper had obviously done his worst to Indie and Amy. They'd turned against him! They were going to destroy him!

"Let's talk about this, huh?" he said kindly to Indie, hoping that somehow, he could get through to him. But Indie had no choice but to stare meanly back at him, with Ratz watching.

"Move it," Amy snapped.

"Amy! It's Mike here, remember me?" Mike hissed desperately.

Amy's reply was to push Mike roughly ahead of her, past Ratz. Mike's legs, still weak, stumbled as he tried to keep his balance.

"Guess they don't like you any more, Mike," Ratz smirked.

Mike managed to glare at him, but panic was rising in him. Indie and Amy seemed to be completely immune to him!

But a huge wave of relief washed over him as Indie sidled out past Ratz and hissed, "It's okay, Mike! I'm fine but Amy's not!"

Now Amy moved jerkily into the corridor, Ratz behind her. She paused for a moment, looking Mike up and down evilly.

"It's show time!" she cackled, sounding horribly like Viper.

Mike's heart stopped. Indie's did likewise. Ratz laughed. "That's good, Amy," he sniggered. Amy smiled back.

"Hey, Ratz," she said suddenly. "What's that?"

She pointed back into the dungeons. Ratz, on reflex, turned to have a look, whereupon Amy lifted her foot and soundly booted him. He landed on his back in the middle of the floor, just in time to see her swinging the dungeon door closed on him.

"You rat!" she said. "I hope you never get out."

She quickly locked the door and then casually dropped the key down a grate in the corridor. It disappeared into the filth.

"Come on," she told an astonished Mike and Indie, as she set off down the corridor. Behind them, they could hear Ratz's outraged howls.

Amy led them fast through the corridors until she saw that

Mike was having difficulty running, his legs wobbling under him. She stopped.

"Take a second to catch your breath," she said kindly, patting his arm.

"You... you were only pretending!" Indie accused.

"Course. I didn't read that chatline at all, I concentrated on a speck of dust on the screen. You didn't really think I was brainwashed, did you?"

"Well *I* did!" Mike offered indignantly between breaths.

"Sorry about that, I guess I got a bit carried away," Amy smiled.

"I must say, there was no call for that shove you gave me," Mike huffed.

"Look, I had to convince Ratz," Amy offered simply. "And sorry Indie, but you weren't doing a great job of it."

Indie now looked indignant. "I thought I was pretty okay!"

Mike interrupted. "We can give out the awards later. Right now, I'm just glad that you're both okay."

He sagged against the wall, Indie watching him worriedly. "Never mind about us. What on earth have they done to YOU?"

Mike rubbed his arms and shoulders. They were sore, but he could feel the strength coming back into them.

"I'm okay."

"Well then, can we please get out of here?" Indie implored.

"But we don't know where the exit is," Amy pointed out.

Mike looked thoughtful. "I'll bet one of those computers upstairs has some kind of a layout of the bunker on it."

"But Viper's in the computer room!"

Amy looked horrified at the thoughts of meeting Viper again. But Mike smiled encouragingly.

"If you could convince ME that you were brainwashed, Amy, I'll bet you could fool Viper that you've carried out his orders."

"What, you mean pretend that I've got you tied up outside?"

"Yep. Ask him if he wants to go out and have a look at me, tied to a cactus. And I'll roar and scream like mad from here. He won't be able to resist."

"What about me?" Indie asked, miffed that he was being left out.

"No offence Indie, but your acting's not great," Mike said sympathetically. "Anyway, you can help me shout and scream."

Another burst of yelling reached them from below – Ratz.

"Time to go, Amy, before Viper discovers Ratz is missing. And good luck."

Amy solemnly shook Indie and Mike's hand, and set off into the blackness. Mike and Indie pressed themselves against the wall, waiting.

"How did you manage to escape the subliminal messages?" Mike whispered.

Indie shrugged. "I just stared at the top of the screen. I might have looked down once or twice, but I'm okay."

Mike peered up the corridor. "Okay, Indie, time to give the performance of a lifetime. ARRGHHH!"

He sounded like he was in desperate pain, even though he was obviously enjoying himself. "Come on Indie, pretend that you've got me tied up!"

Indie joined in, embarrassed. "YOU STAY QUIET, YOU CRITTER!"

Critter? Mike looked askance at Indie. "LET ME GO!"

"Em, NO WAY!" Indie replied, trying to sound authentic. "NOT TILL HELL FREEZES OVER!"

Mike threw his eyes skywards. "Try to be a little more natural," he advised kindly, anxiously looking up the corridor. No sign of anything happening. He hoped that Amy was okay.

"OOOOAAAAHHH!" He let a final blood-curdling roar of feigned pain.

At last, some action. Footsteps were pounding in their direction. He quickly pressed Indie and himself right back against the wall and into the concealing shadows.

"Don't move!" he commanded, just as Viper Virus swept past, Donna on his heels.

"This should be fun," Viper cackled over his shoulder at Donna.

"Depends on your idea of fun," she replied dismissively.

They moved on, bickering, the blackness swallowing them up.

Mike stepped out cautiously from the wall.

"Okay. Coast's clear. Let's go!"

They found Amy sitting triumphantly in Viper's chair in the computer room.

"Well done!" Indie beamed.

"He's gone out to taunt you, Mike," Amy laughed.

Mike carefully locked and bolted the door and then put a chair under the handle for good measure.

"Well he won't find me. Nice work, Amy," he winked, before going swiftly to the nearest computer.

"Now. We need a floor plan of the bunker," he said busily.

"Mike? This might sound stupid, but why don't we just e-mail Mr Broadhead and get out of here?" Indie asked.

Mike grew very still. "It, ah, appears that Mr Broadhead is unable to help us."

"What?"

"Look, I don't know what's happened, but *The Daily Rap* has been shut down and the web site is gone from the Net. Mr Broadhead seems to have packed up and left." Mike tried to keep the bitterness out of his voice.

He still couldn't quite credit that Mr Broadhead had been unable to stop this state of affairs.

"No, not Mr Broadhead," Indie said incredulously.

"It's in the newspapers, okay?" Mike said impatiently.

"Can't you try anyway?" Amy asked.

Mike grumbled under his breath. "We don't have the time for this, but if that's what it takes to convince you…"

With sharp, rather angry punches, he tapped into the Net and searched for *The Daily Rap*'s web site.

"See? I told you. It's gone. Kaput. Mr Broadhead has upped and left us to our own devices."

But he froze as he looked back at the computer screen. There it was! *The Daily Rap*'s web site.

"He hasn't dumped us!" Indie cried.

Mike felt rather foolish. What about *The Rattler*'s headline? Was it all some elaborate joke of Ratz's? He felt even worse that he'd doubted Mr Broadhead…

"This means that we can get out of here this minute!" Amy clapped gleefully.

This was true. They could. Mike decided he could sort out *The Daily Rap*'s apparent demise later. Right now, it was time to check out of Viper's bunker.

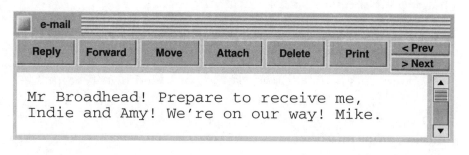

He quickly sent the e-mail and then gestured to Indie and Amy.

"Okay guys, up on the desk here beside me. The minute Mr Broadhead replies, we're outta here."

Indie and Amy gladly scrambled up beside Mike and waited. Then, an answering e-mail flashed up.

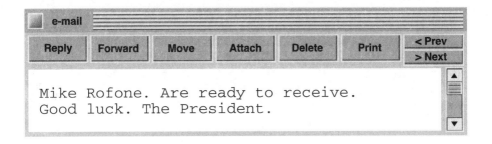

```
  e-mail
  Reply   Forward   Move   Attach   Delete   Print   < Prev
                                                     > Next
```

Mike Rofone. Are ready to receive.
Good luck. The President.

The President? THE PRESIDENT?

"Guys? Am I reading that message right?" Mike asked confused.

"I think so... Wow, the President!" Amy shouted.

They looked at each other in excitement, then towards Indie, who so far, had said nothing.

"Hey, who cares," Indie shrugged, then immediately wondered why he'd said that. "I mean, yeah, it's great," he quickly corrected himself.

Mike Rofone was looking at him strangely.

"Sorry, Mike. I guess I'm tired," Indie said. He *was* tired. Very tired.

Suddenly, the door to the computer room started to shake with a series of blows.

"You tricked me! This time, I'll show NO MERCY!" Viper's voice, from outside the door.

"Quick! Hurry!" Mike hopped into the computer screen, growing tiny as he landed on the Net. He reached out, grabbed Amy's arm and tugged gently. She was sucked through the screen and landed beside Mike.

"Indie, hurry!"

Now, Mike reached out for Indie. But Indie looked distracted.

"Come on, Indie! Viper will burst through the door any second!"

Indie was feeling rather peculiar. And he was also getting very irritated at everybody having a go at Viper. He wasn't that bad a guy, was he?

Indie couldn't quite remember when he'd changed his opinion of Viper, but he felt it was time that somebody stood up for him.

"I don't want to go. I want to stay here," he heard himself saying.

"Indie? Indie, have you lost your marbles?"

Amy's voice sounded as though it were coming through layers and layers of cotton wool.

Then, suddenly, he felt himself grabbed and then he was floating through the air... and PLOP! He landed gently beside Amy and Mike Rofone.

"Indie?" Mike was now saying kindly. "We're going home."

Indie shrugged. As if he could care less. There was only one place he wanted to go. And that was back to his friend, Viper Virus.

CHAPTER 11

Mr Broadhead broke open a bottle of cola.

"It's a celebration!" he enthused, filling paper cups.

The newspaper office was once again buzzing with activity. The staff were back in force, working flat out to get the next edition of *The Daily Rap* onto the stands. It was business as usual.

Mike and Amy sat side by side on Mr Broadhead's desk. He reverently handed each of them a paper cup of cola.

"Boy, I needed that," Amy gasped, having downed the whole lot in one go.

But Mike handed his back.

"No thanks, Mr Broadhead."

"What?" Mr Broadhead was absolutely stunned. "But you're a cola addict!"

"Was," Mike corrected. "But after drinking that cola in Viper's place, with sedatives in it, I don't think I'll ever be able to look a cola in the eye again!"

He looked utterly miserable at this prospect.

"Cheer up, Mike. I always said you drank far too much cola," Mr Broadhead reasoned. "Here. Have a mineral water instead."

"It's not the same," Mike observed sadly.

"Indie! Come over here and join the celebration!" Mr Broadhead shouted.

Indie looked up from where he was slouching around at the back of the office.

"No," he said rudely.

Mike, Amy and Mr Broadhead exchanged worried glances. Indie just hadn't been himself ever since they'd arrived back at the office an hour ago.

"I think he's still a bit shocked after all Viper put us

through," Amy offered quietly.

"Sure. Maybe we'd better just leave him alone for a bit," Mr Broadhead said, glad that there was some explanation.

Mike Rofone wasn't so easily put off. He had the growing suspicion that Viper Virus had just claimed the first of the world's children… He decided to keep a careful eye on Indie.

"Tell me more about the President," he said to Mr Broadhead, who was just dying to be asked.

Mr Broadhead looked terribly important. "Well, as you know, I phoned him up. I said, listen here Mr President, there's something wrong, I said—"

"Yeah, yeah, we've heard what YOU said a million times. But what did the President say?"

Mr Broadhead looked put out, but then his good humour came back as he re-told the story of how the President had known nothing about the entire affair and had been shocked to hear of it. "And he's pulling out all the stops, Mike! As we speak, a special task force is on its way to the desert. They're going to surround the bunker so that Viper and his cronies can't escape, and they're going to strike in about two hours' time! He ordered the Secretary of Defence to give it number one priority!"

Mr Broadhead was flushed with success. Mike nodded slowly, pleased.

"So Viper's caught."

"You bet. And just as soon as they can locate the power supply in the desert, they'll cut his computer system off so that he can't do any more damage on the Net."

"What about the disk?"

"They're going to destroy it the second they get their hands on it!"

Mike was relieved.

Mr Broadhead paused only to wet his throat with cola before continuing.

"He made Bud and Chet return the chip and then he

arrived here in person – in person, Mike! Arrived by his private jet!"

Mike thought Mr Broadhead would collapse with the excitement of it all.

"Wow! You actually got to meet the President?" Amy asked in awe.

"Don't encourage him, Amy," Mike said in disgust. He was a little out of sorts that *he'd* done all the hard work, yet it was Mr Broadhead who'd gotten to meet the President.

Mr Broadhead was now on a roll. "Sure did. We shared a cup of coffee and I told him about some of my dreams!"

"Oh boy," Mike groaned.

"He was very interested," Mr Broadhead huffed. "But you want to know the best thing?"

"What?" Amy asked.

"The best thing," Mr Broadhead said, his voice cracking with emotion, "is that he's coming back!"

"Steady on, Mr Broadhead," Mike said. But this was exciting news indeed. "To the newspaper office?"

"Yes!" Mr Broadhead squealed. "You won't believe why, Mike. You'll never guess!"

"Oh for goodness' sake, tell me!" Mike said, with mock impatience.

Mr Broadhead took centre stage and spread his arms wide. "He's going to give us a commendation for public service!"

"WHAT?" Amy and Mike chorused in disbelief.

"He's so pleased that we stopped Viper that we're all going to get an award! Me, you, Indie, Amy and *The Daily Rap!*"

Mr Broadhead, having finally gotten it all out of his system, collapsed into his leather chair.

"A commendation! Me!" Amy said, totally stunned.

"Oh boy!" Mike couldn't keep the wide grin off his face. An award! This was better than a scoop any day!

"He's coming back this afternoon!" Mr Broadhead announced. "So you're all to go home and get all spruced up and be back here at three sharp!"

Mike Rofone suddenly grew serious. "He'll get some shock when he learns that Viper Virus has been stockpiling nuclear missiles."

Mr Broadhead nodded. HE'D gotten some shock when Mike had told him about the more sinister contents of Viper's bunker.

"I hope they destroy them," Amy said.

"You bet they will," Mr Broadhead nodded. "Looks like you all stumbled on to something pretty scary there. That Viper. I never guessed he'd be prepared to go so far."

"Viper's capable of anything," Mike observed cynically.

"Imagine! The President!" Mr Broadhead was off again. "Here in this office! Drinking coffee with me!"

"It's far from drinking coffee we were, stuck in Viper's bunker!" Mike returned, getting tired of Mr Broadhead's boasting.

Mr Broadhead looked hurt. "But I got you out, didn't I? And you thought I'd abandoned you! There's trust for you!"

"Sorry about that," Mike said contritely. "But I didn't know what else to think."

"But we knew you'd come through in the end, Mr Broadhead," Amy added, and received a large smile of thanks.

Mr Broadhead slapped the desk in a business-like fashion. "Right. Mike, you'd better get Indie and Amy home right away, and I'll see you all back here at three."

"Sure," said Mike, casting another worried look in Indie's direction.

Indie was watching them very coldly.

"And later," Mr Broadhead continued, "I want you to start writing your exclusive for the front page of tomorrow's edition of *The Daily Rap*. It'll be the biggest scoop of your career, Mike!"

Mr Broadhead was now totally shattered after the events of the day and promptly fell asleep.

"Come on, Amy. Time to get you home," Mike said, getting to his feet.

"Mike? Can't I just hang out here until it's time to meet the President?" she pleaded.

Mike looked at her incredulously. "Amy, your parents are bound to miss you by now. Like I told Indie, time moves much faster on the Net, but you've still been gone a while now."

"Ha!" she scoffed. "They still won't have missed me. Sometimes, I stay out all day on purpose and nobody ever says anything to me."

Mike watched her curiously. "They probably don't want to crowd you, Amy. But you shouldn't try to make them worried."

"Why not? It's the only way they take any notice of me!" she said defiantly, but her eyes were a little too bright.

"Well now, that's just plain silly, isn't it, Amy?" Mike said sternly.

Amy scuffed her shoe on the carpet.

"Hmmm. I think you need to have a chat with your parents," he advised.

"A chat? With my parents? Nobody ever chats with their parents. What would I say?"

"What you told me."

Amy looked highly sceptical. "Maybe."

"I think you should do it now, Amy," he said, leading her towards his computer. "The minute I drop you home. Hey, Indie! Want a ride home?"

But Indie just glared at him from the back of the office.

"What's up, Indie?" Mike asked, concerned, going over to him.

"Nothing," Indie snapped and stared at the floor.

"You tired?"

Indie refused to answer.

"You want to go home?" Mike asked.

Indie nodded curtly and followed Mike back to his desk.

Mike watched him carefully as he hopped into his computer. He'd have to get to the bottom of this...

"Yikes!" Amy gulped, as she landed on the Net beside Mike. Then Indie was beside her, and Mike Rofone was reaching out through the computer screen and e-mailing them right across America.

First stop was Amy. She was safely deposited in her bedroom in Toronto, with a promise to be back at the newspaper office at three in time to meet the President.

"Hey, buddy?" Mike looked across at Indie. They were floating at speed somewhere over the Atlantic ocean. Dublin Bay was coming up fast.

"Anything you want to get off your chest?"

But Indie merely shook his head. Mike decided that he had to find out for certain whether Indie had been influenced by Viper's subliminal messages, or whether there was something else wrong.

"Ah! Here we are!" he said with a false cheer, as they landed in Indie's computer. Through the screen, he could see the Johnsons' living-room.

Indie made for the screen immediately.

"Hang on a second, Indie."

"What," Indie said tonelessly.

"You okay about Viper? Like, he didn't scare you too much?"

Indie turned and looked straight at him. "No. Viper doesn't scare me at all. I like him. He's cool."

Then he turned his back rudely on Mike and jumped out of his computer screen. Mike could see him walking out of the living-room and slamming the door.

Mike's worst suspicions were confirmed. Viper had Indie firmly in his clutches. The question was, could he cure him before it was too late?

"What? WHAT?" Mr Broadhead mumbled sleepily, as Mike roughly jerked him awake.

"I'm going back to the bunker!"

"I beg your pardon?"

"Indie's brainwashed!"

Mr Broadhead gulped. "That's terrible! But why are you going back to the bunker?"

Mike was frantic. "If that disk brainwashed him, then only that disk can undo the damage! There must be a reverse command on it. I'll have to get the disk, find out the command, and use it on Indie!"

Mr Broadhead looked confused. "But the President has instructed the army to destroy the disk! They should be striking any moment now!"

Mike slapped the table sharply. "Exactly! And if I don't get to that disk before the army does, Indie will be brainwashed forever!"

This sunk in with Mr Broadhead. "My God, you're right! We can't let them destroy that disk!"

"We have to move fast."

"I'm coming with you," Mr Broadhead said with spirit. "There's no telling what Viper could do to you."

Mike shook his head firmly.

"No. No offence, but you're a... well, a PERSON, Mr Broadhead."

"Of course I'm a person! What did you think I was?"

Mike tried to explain it a little better. "But I'm a microphone. Whatever chance I have of slipping in undetected, I haven't a hope with you in tow."

Mr Broadhead was secretly relieved, but managed to conceal it.

"Right. I'm gone," Mike announced, jumping up on to the desk.

"Good luck, Mike," Mr Broadhead said solemnly. "I'll tell the President that you're sorry you missed his visit."

"What?"

"Well, it's almost three. You won't be here." Mr Broadhead looked pained.

Mike was still for a moment, thinking of his glorious meeting with the President, his award for bravery, the golden handshake… and then he put it firmly out of his mind. It wasn't to be, it seemed.

"Hey, there'll be other meetings with the President," he managed to joke, even though both of them knew that there wouldn't. But Mike swallowed his disappointment. He had work to do. Hard, dangerous work, where he would come up against Viper Virus for the last time.

"Indie! Where on earth have you been?" his mother cried, worry etched all over her face.

"You've been gone nearly all morning!" his father joined in, relieved that finally Indie was home.

Indie stared blankly at his computer, which he'd hauled back to his bedroom without bothering to ask permission.

"Indie? I asked you where you've been," his mother said, annoyance taking over from her worry.

"Mind your own business," Indie replied loftily.

He heard her sharp intake of breath and didn't care.

"INDIE JOHNSON!" his father roared. "How dare you speak to your mother like that!"

Indie now swung around in his chair and glared meanly at them. "Indie, where have you been?" he mimicked. "Indie, you've been gone all morning! Indie, you must have been the one who stole that rhubarb tart, who broke that window, who sprayed graffiti on the bike shed!"

His parents took a step back, speechless.

"Well I'm fed up with you watching my every move, and blaming me for things I didn't do!" he shouted. "And if I want to stay out all morning, I'll stay out all morning! It doesn't mean I've done something wrong!"

His parents gaped at him, aghast. Then, his father slowly led his mother out of the room.

At the door, he turned back.

"You'll stay in here until you're more yourself, young man." But his father didn't sound so much angry as downright shaken.

The door slammed. Indie turned back to his computer, grinning. Viper would be proud of him for being so rude and defiant.

He got on-line and immediately composed an e-mail.

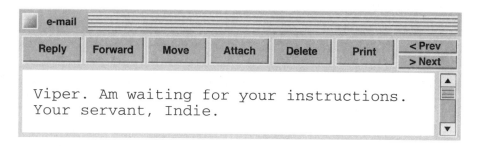

He sat back and waited for Viper's reply. He looked forward to carrying out Viper's orders, whatever they may be. And he was dying to get back to the bunker. He missed it, with the rats and the filth and the darkness. He even missed Ratz. He thought that they might become friends.

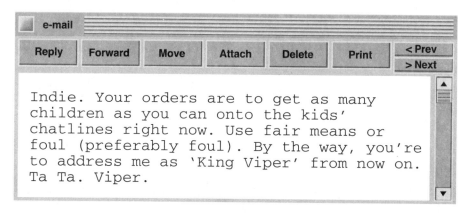

Indie felt a little tingle of anticipation. Then he busily went to work on his computer, e-mailing every single friend and acquaintance he could think of. He felt sorry for them, not having Viper as a friend. He'd be very glad to introduce them.

CHAPTER 12

Viper Virus was splayed in a chair, motionless, eyes closed. His pet rats skulked at his feet, guarding him.

"I think he's asleep."

"You sure?"

Donna and Ratz were huddled in a corner, watching him fearfully. He certainly appeared to be asleep, but with Viper, you could never be sure.

"Maybe his little fit tired him out," Donna whispered.

Once he'd discovered that Indie, Amy and Mike Rofone had escaped, Viper had flown into a rage the like of which Donna and Ratz had never seen before.

Demented, he'd stormed through the dungeons, twisting bars out of shape and ripping up the concrete floor. Then he'd torn every single door off its hinges, one by one. In the computer room, he'd hurled every last computer to the floor. Finally, like some ugly whirlwind, he'd taken to the air, and flown haphazardly at the walls, crashing into them and leaving huge craters behind.

When the bunker was reduced to a pile of rubble, he had turned his wrath on Donna and Ratz.

But just as he'd been about to choke Ratz, one of the smashed computers had suddenly jumped to life, a message becoming visible on its cracked screen – a message from Indie Johnson. It appeared that Viper's subliminal messages had worked after all.

Viper had immediately been restored to good humour. He'd released Ratz, e-mailed Indie with instructions, then had apparently fallen asleep.

"What's he going to do next?" Ratz now whispered to Donna.

"I don't know," she hissed back. "But I'm not waiting to find out!"

She quietly stood up. Ratz jumped to his feet too.

"You're not leaving me with HIM!"

Thrown together by the need to survive, they'd become quite friendly.

Donna took Ratz's arm.

"We'll go into the desert and make a run for it," she murmured. "We mightn't last long out there, but I suspect we've a better chance than down here."

Ratz suddenly looked furtive. "You go on ahead. I gotta do something first."

Donna was suspicious. "What?"

Ratz didn't answer. Instead, he eased towards his tape recorder which lay on the ground beside a cracked computer.

"Forget it," Donna hissed.

Ratz glared at her. "I just gotta get the tape out of it, that's all. For my exclusive."

Donna looked uneasily at her feet. "Ah, it's gone. The tape."

"WHAT?"

"I took the tape. Viper had already sold his exclusive, Ratz. He never had any intention of giving you your scoop."

Ratz was stunned at this treachery. "That SCUM!"

"Shut up! Do you want to wake him?" Donna hissed angrily. "Now forget about your career! I'm going and you'd better decide whether you're coming with me or not!"

It didn't take Ratz long to make up his mind. He scurried after Donna.

"All right, all right!"

Soundlessly, they tip-toed towards the door.

Twenty feet to go… ten feet… five…

"Going somewhere?"

They whirled around to find Viper wide awake and watching them lazily.

"Uh–uh–uh–" was all Ratz could manage in his terror.

"Indeed we were," Donna agreed, quickly recovering. "We were going to see if you'd left any part of the bunker standing, Viper."

Viper looked puzzled, then it all came back to him. "Ah yes, my little tantrum. Sorry about that. Sometimes I let my emotions get the better of me."

"So we'll just go and survey the damage," Donna said, quickly pushing Ratz ahead of her. They might still have a chance…

"Don't bother," Viper barked, and Donna's heart plunged into her expensive designer shoes. "We'll have to leave the bunker in any case. I'm sure Mike Rofone hasn't been idle since he escaped. I wouldn't be at all surprised if the police are planning a little visit sometime soon."

"I'll go and pack then," Donna tried desperately.

"Oh, there's no hurry, is there?" Viper asked softly.

He watched her through hooded eyes and Donna had the creepy suspicion that he knew exactly what she was up to.

"First, we've our final experiment to conduct," he murmured. "Indie has very kindly rounded up thousands of kids on the chatlines. I think it's time to convert them, what do you think?"

Donna and Ratz exchanged defeated glances. "Very good, Viper," they chorused dully.

Neither wanted to have anything more to do with Viper's evil plans. There were some things more important than big scoops and well-paid PR jobs – things like their own skins, for example.

"Wonderful," Viper said, knowing full well that neither Ratz nor Donna were on his side any longer. But he didn't care.

"Foot soldiers," he murmured to the rats at his feet. "To be dispensed with when they have no further use."

Donna caught the tail-end of this and froze. She knew now that she would never leave the bunker alive...

Viper glided forward to the cracked computer that was still working. The rats scurried after him.

"Come," he smiled at Donna and Ratz. Meekly, they took up positions beside the rats.

With a flourish, Viper produced the disk containing the subliminal messages and slid it into the battered disk drive of the computer.

"Ten... nine... eight..." he chanted. "Come on Donna, Ratz! Let's do a countdown! This is a wonderful moment!"

Ratz and Donna stared at him unenthusiastically.

"COUNT!" Viper snarled. "You will not spoil my moment! Seven... six..."

Ratz and Donna exchanged fearful glances, then began to chant in unison.

"Five... four... three... two... one!"

"BLAST OFF!" Viper screamed triumphantly, stabbing at a key on the computer. The screen flickered erratically as the disk emptied its terrible messages onto the chatlines.

Ratz, Donna and the sewer rats waited, breaths held, for what seemed like an eternity.

Viper lolled idly in his chair, sharpening his fingernails with a nail file, as if he were rather bored by it all.

"How will we know they've worked?" Ratz eventually asked.

"Find out if I've any e-mail, there's a good fellow," Viper said sweetly.

Trembling, Ratz took over at the keyboard.

"Yeah, Boss. There's... my God! There's thousands of e-mails!"

Viper couldn't conceal his excitement.

"Read one to me!" he commanded.

Ratz cleared his throat and read. "Viper. You're the greatest. Phillipe here in France."

Viper was flushed with pleasure. "Donna! Read me another one!"

Donna peered at the screen. "Viper Virus. Got your message and I'm thrilled that you've chosen me. I'm ready to carry out your instructions. Mo in China."

"It's worked! I'm a star!" Viper swooned. He turned to his pet rats, who eyed him with dislike. "I'm a star, my pretties! I'm King—"

Suddenly, the computer screen emitted a cough and went blank.

"Darned thing," Viper growled, and soundly thumped it.

The screen went very fuzzy, then, slowly, the fuzz started to take shape.

Ratz and Donna squinted hard. Viper bared his teeth. The shape became more and more distinct... it was Mike Rofone.

"Soooo. We've got company," Viper murmured softly.

Inside the computer, Mike Rofone's fists were curled into tight balls, and his stomach was quivering with nerves. He glared out at Viper, who was grinning back at him. He decided to wipe the smile off his face.

"Guess what, Viper? You're surrounded by the army, the air force and the federal police. They're about to barge in here any second now. You'll never see the light of day again!"

But strangely, Viper didn't appear at all annoyed. Instead, he threw back his head and laughed, giving Mike an eyeful of his black, chipped teeth.

Mike grew more nervous. There was something going on that he didn't know about...

Finally, Viper wiped the tears of laughter from his eyes. "You're too late, Mike," he giggled. "I've just flooded the Net with my messages. The kids are on my side now. You're – too – late!"

Mike was stunned. His task had just gotten a thousand times more difficult. Not only did he have to save Indie, but all the other kids too!

"I don't believe you!" he scoffed at Viper, even though he did. "Come in here and tell me to my face!"

Viper chuckled more. "Oh no, I don't think so. You'd like that, wouldn't you, Mike? You'd like to get me on to the Net so you could have the upper hand."

Once again, Viper was one step ahead of him, Mike groaned inwardly.

"Why don't you come out here to me?" Viper invited with a wicked smile.

Mike froze. No way did he want to go into the bunker again. He couldn't hope to win against Viper on solid ground.

"Scared, huh?" Viper goaded. "Can't handle it? Well then, I guess you'd better scoot off back to your newspaper office like a good boy."

Mike was incensed. He told himself to keep a clear head, that there was no point in letting Viper get to him...

"No, Viper," he managed calmly.

Viper suddenly looked crafty. Then, with lethal speed, he flung out a bat wing and grabbed Ratz by the scruff of the neck.

"AAHHHH!" Ratz roared in terror, as Viper opened his jaws and bared his teeth, poised to sink them into the soft flesh at the back of his neck.

"Come out and save Ratz," Viper challenged Mike. Mike forced himself to smile. Viper was calling his bluff.

"Come on," Viper teased, his teeth inching down to Ratz's neck. "You're such a do-gooder, aren't you, Mike? Well then, SAVE RATZ!"

Ratz's face convulsed as Viper's pointed teeth touched his skin. Mike stiffened, wanting to rush forward and stop this, but still he forced himself to stay put. It was a trap.

"Mike! Mike you gotta save me! He's gonna kill me!" Ratz was screaming now, Viper's fangs penetrating his flesh.

Mike choked down the urge to dash to the rescue. If he held out long enough, maybe Viper would let Ratz go…

"Mike. He'll do it. He'll kill him." Donna looked him straight in the eye.

This was the final straw. He couldn't contain himself any longer. He hated Ratz with a vengeance, but he was still human, wasn't he?

With a great jump, he propelled himself from the Net and through the computer screen, and landed squarely on Viper's desk.

"You let him go now!" he roared, as he picked up a broken computer screen and prepared to throw it straight at Viper.

But Viper immediately forgot all about Ratz. He tossed him casually aside.

"I don't want Ratz. I want YOU," he hissed softly. "You fell for it, you idiot."

Mike Rofone does not take kindly to being called an idiot, especially as he's not one. He looked quickly at Donna and Ratz and the seven vicious-looking black rats.

"Why don't you get rid of your lackeys, Viper, and take me on by yourself. Or do you need them for moral support?" He made his voice deliberately insulting.

Viper grew red in the face. Several veins popped high in his cheeks.

"I don't need anybody!" he managed, his voice cracking with rage. He pointed at Donna and Ratz. "Get out and don't come back until I've finished with Mike Rofone."

Donna and Ratz needed no further instructions. They sped out the door, the seven rats hot on their heels.

Now, once again, it was just Viper Virus and Mike Rofone. They stared at each other, neither blinking.

"We've got to stop meeting like this," Viper smiled.

"Save your breath, Viper. You'll need it," Mike snapped.

The smile slid off Viper's face.

"If that's the way you want it... Do your worst Mike. Because you can be sure I'll do mine."

With that, he rose up, his bat wings fully extended. He hung in the air, poised, his hair standing on end and his teeth and pointy fingernails bared and ready for attack.

Mike Rofone had no wings, no fangs and no fingernails (right now, he was wishing that he'd managed to quit biting them). He had only his wits in the face of this awful creature.

The air suddenly moved. Viper swooped, quick as lightening.

On reflex, Mike flung himself to the ground. He could feel Viper's nails skinning his back, but not quite getting a grip.

"Missed!" he taunted, but his bravado disappeared as Viper now surged downwards again from the ceiling, saliva dripping from his jaw.

"This one's for Blackrattler!" he screeched, as he threw Mike flat against a wall. Mike slid to the floor, the breath knocked out of him.

He just had time to scramble to his feet as Viper came at him a third time.

"Feeling tired?" Viper cackled, as he hung comfortably in the furthest corner of the room. "Because I'm just starting to enjoy myself."

Mike was now very scared. He was no match for this flying maniac.

"Woah!" he squeaked as Viper plunged again, like some obscenely overgrown bird.

"GOTCHA!" Viper howled victoriously, as his feet dug firmly into Mike's back.

Mike's heart jolted painfully as he was suddenly lifted into the air by Viper. The claws embedded in his back tightened painfully as he watched with horror the floor getting further and further away and the ceiling approaching fast.

"I think we'll have a little fun, how about that?" Viper shouted with glee.

Then he let loose with his flying powers.

Mike's stomach threatened to empty itself as Viper did somersaults and figures-of-eight, hair-raising plunges and death-defying spins.

The room tilted crazily around Mike, making him dizzy.

"Had enough yet?" Viper laughed.

"No!" Mike managed, and steeled himself as they plummeted downwards... the floor was getting nearer and nearer... Mike shut his eyes and waited for the bang.

At the last moment, Viper angled upwards. "Hmmm, that was a close one," he giggled hysterically.

I'm finished, Mike thought. Absolutely finished. Once he's done playing, he'll probably crash-land into the ceiling and that'll be the end of me...

He shot a fearful look at the ceiling. And then he saw it. A huge, thick blanket of cobweb, hanging from corner to corner, like a large dust-encrusted hammock. Viper was flying precariously close to the cobweb, but managing to avoid it.

Mike took a deep breath as Viper, screaming with laughter, did a nose-dive to the floor again.

How strong is the cobweb? Mike frantically wondered. Can it hold Viper? It was worth a try...

"I'm bored, Viper!" he shouted upwards. "You're going to have to do better than this!"

As he'd expected, Viper stiffened with rage, and started to fly even more manically around the middle of the room.

"Scared of heights?" Mike taunted.

"Not unless you are!" Viper snapped, and as Mike had hoped, surged upwards, towards the ceiling. Higher, he prayed, go higher, Viper! There was the cobweb now... just a little higher, Viper!

"AWWWAHHHHH!"

Suddenly, they were hanging motionless.

"What's happened?" Viper bellowed in panic. Mike craned

his neck. Viper's bat wings were firmly entangled in the cobweb. He hoped that it was strong enough to contain him.

He decided he'd lessen the weight. He aimed a kick at Viper's soft overweight belly.

"Ohhhh," Viper groaned, and stiffened his legs. His feet released Mike.

Mike tumbled to the ground and lay there for a moment, wondering if anything was broken.

"I think I'm okay," he said, and got slowly to his feet. He looked upwards where Viper was struggling frantically against the cobweb. The cobweb creaked. Mike had a suspicion that it wouldn't hold Viper for long. He had to work fast.

"Ratz! Donna!" he roared. Silence. Had they deserted the bunker?

But no. The door creaked open and the pair, trembling, peeked in. They saw with relief and astonishment, Viper hanging from the roof.

"Ratz!" Viper commanded loudly. "Cut me down!"

Ratz gave Viper an ugly look. "No way, Boss."

"It's an ORDER, Ratz!" Viper's voice would curdle blood.

"I might've helped you if you hadn't done me out of my scoop!" Ratz shouted back.

Viper was stunned. "Donna!" he blubbered. "Help me!"

"Shove off, Viper," she said casually. "Mike, what can we do to help?"

"Where's the disk! Quick!" Mike said urgently, as the cobweb creaked again.

"In the computer."

Donna quickly got the disk. "Any copies?" Mike asked.

"Yes. Ratz made some."

Ratz looked sheepish. "Uh, no, actually. I forgot."

"Good," Mike nodded, as he hopped up onto the desk, the disk safely in his pocket. "See ya, kids."

"Don't leave us here!" Ratz and Donna quivered as the

cobweb started to give away under Viper's thrashing. Viper howled, as he started to bite through the cobweb, shredding it with his fangs.

Mike's gaze grew cold as he looked down at Donna and Ratz. For two pins, he'd leave the pair of them here with Viper. They deserved it, after all they'd done.

But again, his better nature surfaced, and he simply couldn't.

"All right. Hurry up!" he snapped, not bothering to conceal his dislike. "The army's gonna cut off the power supply to the bunker any second now, and if we don't get out of here soon, we'll be trapped with Viper."

That was enough to propel Donna and Ratz onto the desk beside Mike.

"Aha!" Viper roared triumphantly, as he freed a wing from the cobweb.

"Time to split," Mike said, jumping into the computer screen. Roughly, he reached out and dragged Donna with him. Then he hauled Ratz in after her. Keeping a careful eye on both, he reached out through the screen one last time to key in commands that would e-mail them out.

Viper Virus suddenly fell to the floor, the cobweb falling after him.

"Ciao, Viper," Mike smiled nastily, and a second later, disappeared from the screen. Almost immediately, the computer went completely dead and all the lights in the bunker went out as the army cut off the power supply.

Viper Virus sat on the floor in the dark, smothered by dusty cobwebs and surrounded by his seven pet rats. He started to scream, ear-splitting shrieks of rage and anguish. He screamed and screamed until his face grew red and his throat raw. Eventually, his voice went and he could only manage a few pathetic croaks.

Now, he could hear the bunker's trapdoor crashing in upstairs.

By the sounds of it, he'd have an entire platoon down on top of him any second. But he didn't jump to his feet or try to hide. By the time they found the computer room, Viper intended to be long gone.

"Right, my pretties. Fancy a little stroll?" He could just make out the rats in the darkness.

The rats hated exercise and shook their heads vigorously in unison.

"Tough," spat Viper. "Because we're leaving."

The rats drew back, scared, as Viper got to his feet and spread his wings. Before their very eyes, he suddenly started to shrink. His wings slowly grew into tiny paws and coarse, black hair started to sprout from every pore on his skin. His eyes became tiny and beady and two small ears protruded from his forehead. Finally, his nose grew into a tiny snout and he let forth a squeak. He had transformed himself into a rat. Then he turned tail and scampered across the computer room towards the door. The seven pet rats obediently followed.

Out in the desert, a big burly army corporal stood scanning the horizon intently. He shuddered in disgust as eight filthy black rats appeared from a nearby sewer, hissed at him, then scampered off into the desert. The corporal pressed a button on his walkie-talkie.

"No sign of him out here, Colonel."

CHAPTER 13

The big solemn garda grunted in satisfaction as he snapped handcuffs onto Jason Ratz.

"Ouch!" Ratz grumbled. "They're too tight!"

"That's the least of your worries, buster," the garda said grimly, and Ratz was quiet. The garda then handcuffed Donna too.

"What do you want me to do with 'em, Mike?" he said over his shoulder.

Mike Rofone was sprawled casually in a chair in the middle of the police station in Dublin. He looked Donna and Ratz up and down in disgust.

"Chuck them into a cell and keep them safe. I'm betting that at least half a dozen countries, including America, will be howling for their blood."

Ratz cringed. Donna went pale.

"Yeah," the garda solemnly agreed. "I'd say they're looking at life imprisonment."

Ratz gave a horrified moan. Donna almost fell out of her seat in shock.

Both totally missed the sly wink which passed between Mike and the garda.

"Hey," the garda said, as though the thought had just occurred to him. "Don't they still have hanging in some states in America?"

At this, Ratz made a wild choking noise. Donna's eyes almost popped out of her head.

"Sure do," Mike said with zest. "Mind you, some of them opt for lethal injection, or the electric chair."

The garda managed to look surprised. "Really? I'd say that hurts like hell."

Now Ratz was almost in convulsions. Donna started to pray loudly under her breath. Mike Rofone decided that they'd had enough.

"But, of course," he said to the garda, "they're always more lenient on people who admit that they've done wrong, and try to make it all right."

Out of the corner of his eye, he could see a flicker of hope in Donna's eyes. Ratz sat up straighter.

"Yeah," the garda agreed. "All depends on how cooperative they are."

"We'll help if we can. We'll do anything!" Donna implored.

"Whatever you want, you got it!" Ratz chimed in fervently.

Mike faced them for the first time. "Okay. I want the secret command which will reverse the subliminal messages on the disk."

Donna and Ratz immediately looked petrified again. "We couldn't do that. If Viper ever found out, he'd... he'd..." Donna couldn't even imagine what Viper would do.

"Anything else Mike, ask us anything else and you got it. But not the secret command," Ratz begged.

Mike stood and looked at them with contempt.

"Lock them up, garda!"

The garda rattled a bunch of keys. "Just so happens that I got a little room in one of my cells. With a couple of mass murderers. On your feet."

Silence, as Donna and Ratz exchanged more wild glances. They decided that it simply wasn't worth it.

"We'll tell you," Donna mumbled.

"Yeah," Ratz agreed.

Mike Rofone thrust a piece of paper at them. "Write it down. And I'm warning you, if you give me the wrong command, you'll be very, very sorry, won't they garda?"

The garda managed to conceal a smile. He hadn't had so

much excitement in his little police station since he'd arrested Rudolph The Red-Nosed Reindeer for speeding.

Indie Johnson was staring at his computer screen, zombie-like. He'd been like this for hours and hours.

Now, his eyes felt heavy and a headache thumped dully at the back of his brain. But still, he made himself read the chatline, on which kids from all over the world were singing Viper's praises.

King Viper, they were calling him. The chosen one. Vowing to support him in his world coup...

Suddenly, a head protruded into the middle of the text.

Indie blinked. He shook his head vigorously from side to side as though trying to clear it. He was very confused.

"Mike Rofone?" his tongue felt thick and cumbersome.

"Indie? Mind if I come into your bedroom?" Mike was watching him carefully. Indie knew, somewhere in the back of his mind, that he should hate Mike Rofone... destroy him if he got the chance... but somehow, he couldn't.

"Yeah. But only for a minute," he heard himself mumbling.

Now, Mike was beside him, and putting something into his disk drive.

"What are you doing?"

"Sshhh... watch the screen."

Obediently, Indie went back to reading the screen. He was vaguely aware of Mike typing something on his keyboard.

Suddenly, the screen was spewing up different messages. Indie saw several bright lights flashing in front of his eyes and then his headache disappeared. It was like a great weight had been lifted from his brain.

He sat stock still, watching Mike in confusion.

"How are you feeling?" Mike asked, looking concerned.

Indie thought about this. "I'm not sure," he said slowly.

"What happened, Mike? Everything is kind of a blur."

"I think those subliminal messages got to you, Indie."

"WHAT? But I didn't even read the chatline!"

Mike shrugged. "You didn't have to. I've just been through the programme on the disk, and it seems that the subliminal messages weren't in the text, but at the top of the screen."

Indie's eyes widened. "In the words LIVE CHAT?"

Mike nodded.

"That was the only thing I watched," Indie groaned.

"Well, you got the full whack then. He really got to you, Indie."

It was all coming back to Indie slowly... his rudeness to Mike and Amy and Mr Broadhead... his devotion to Viper Virus, of all people... and his blatant backchat to his parents.

"And worse!" he yelped. "I helped put hundreds of kids on the Net! They're all under Viper's influence!"

Mike slid the disk from Indie's computer and waved it triumphantly. "Not for long."

"That's the disk? You went back to the bunker and got it?"

Mike looked modest. "Sure did. I made Ratz give me the reverse command. I used them on you first, to make sure they worked. But now I'm going to flood the Net with them, so the rest of the kids should be all right."

Indie looked immensely relieved. "And Viper? What about him? Will he come after us again?"

"No. I think Viper's out of action," Mike said with satisfaction.

Indie looked mean. "Good! That scum!"

Now, Mike knew that Indie definitely was okay. Busily, he put the disk back into Indie's computer, and prepared to undo Viper's damage.

"Mike?" Indie said meekly. "I'm sorry I was so horrible earlier. I didn't mean it, honest. You've been great, rescuing us from the bunker and saving me, and helping the rest of those kids."

"All in a day's work," Mike said bashfully.

"So that's the end of it all?" Indie said, a little sadly. "No more excitement, or adventures?"

"Well, not quite," Mike said, with a big grin. "The President, remember him?"

"Yes."

He's given us all a personal commendation for our work in stopping Viper!"

"Wow!"

Mike regretfully thought of the President's visit, and how he'd missed it. His fifteen minutes of fame. Ah well. He'd still get his award, even if it wasn't in person.

"Want to come back to the newspaper office and collect our awards?" he asked Indie.

Indie's face lit up, but just as quickly, his excitement died.

"I said some pretty awful things to my parents. I'd say I'll be grounded for the rest of my life, Mike."

Mike thought on this for a minute. "You could apologise. They'll know soon enough about Viper's subliminal messages. It'll be all over *The Daily Rap* in the morning."

Indie looked more down. "I don't know if that'll be enough. I think I need to convince them that I haven't done anything wrong."

Mike's fingers, busy keying in the reverse commands, suddenly grew still.

"Remember the bike shed graffiti?"

"Will I ever forget," Indie said sourly.

"Before I give these kids their own minds back, I think we should conduct a little experiment."

Now Indie was interested. "What experiment."

Mike was grinning to himself. He quickly typed a message onto the chatline.

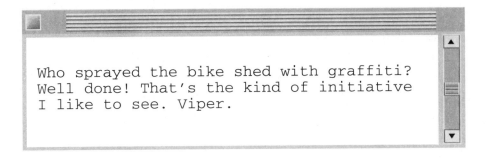

Who sprayed the bike shed with graffiti?
Well done! That's the kind of initiative
I like to see. Viper.

Indie was stunned at this piece of brilliance. "Will they answer?"

Mike shrugged. "Maybe. Maybe not. Depends on if they're still on the Net."

They held their breaths and waited. And at the bottom of the chatline page, a message came back.

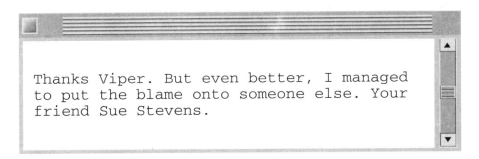

Thanks Viper. But even better, I managed
to put the blame onto someone else. Your
friend Sue Stevens.

Sue Stevens! Indie was agog. Sue Stevens was the most innocent-looking girl in the whole world, with big angelic eyes and cute curly hair. Adults tended to pat her on the head and coo in delight. Sue, of course, lapped it up.

"Who would have thought!?" Indie breathed in awe. Appearances definitely could deceive. Wait until he told his parents.

"There's the proof," Mike said with satisfaction, then quickly tapped a key, sending the reverse commands far and wide across the Net. Two minutes later, the chatlines were busier than ever, with kids swapping insulting remarks about Viper.

"It's worked! They all hate Viper again!" Indie cried, thumping Mike on the back proudly.

"Steady on," Mike coughed. "Now, I'd better get back to the newspaper office. You want to come or not?"

Indie stood. "Yeah. But I've got to apologise to my parents first."

"Good luck."

Indie paused briefly in thought. "You know, some of the things I said to them when I was under Viper's influence, I meant them. About them always looking over my shoulder and stuff. You know, not trusting me."

With resolve, he set off out of the bedroom. Mike yawned loudly, not bothering to cover his mouth with his hand. He decided after the last couple of hectic and hair-raising days, he deserved a holiday.

"Barbados," he announced. "That's where I want to go. And I think you should pay."

Mr Broadhead was incredulous. "I can't pay for holidays for all my staff!"

"But I'm special," Mike said sniffed.

He and Indie were back in the newspaper office. To his surprise, Amy was there as well.

Puzzled, he asked, "What are you still doing here? Didn't you get your award?"

But Amy merely smiled mysteriously and didn't answer. Suddenly, she leaned in to him. "Guess what my parents did?"

"So you took my advice and talked to them?"

"No."

Mike was disappointed. He thought he'd done a great job of advising Amy.

"I didn't need to. They've grounded me! For a whole week!" Amy looked absolutely thrilled. "So you see, they did miss me!"

"And guess what?" Indie piped up. "My parents decided that I shouldn't be grounded any more unless they can prove I did something wrong!"

Mike watched as Indie and Amy grinned in delight at each other. Kids, he thought. He'd just never understand them.

"Say, Mr Broadhead?" he asked. "Where's my award?"

Mr Broadhead looked vague. "Huh? Oh, you weren't here, and the President didn't mention your name. I, ah, I didn't want to press him about it."

Mike Rofone was hurt and shocked. He'd done all the work and now, no award! And all because he had been out risking his life, chasing Viper!

"Oh. I see," he choked. It just wasn't fair!

"You can have a look at mine, if you like," Mr Broadhead boasted. "But first, will you get on with that scoop? You're way behind!"

Mike slumped miserably at his desk, turning his computer on.

Across the office he could see Mr Broadhead huddling with Indie and Amy, giggling and whispering with them.

Slowly, he grew annoyed, then furious. He was totally taken for granted around here!

Not a word of thanks for his efforts, never mind an award! Everybody seemed to have ended up happy except him.

He stood up abruptly. His article could wait until later. *Everything* could wait until later.

"Mike? Where are you going?" Mr Broadhead said suspiciously.

"Out!" Mike said curtly, his voice sounding a little high-pitched.

He stormed out, coming up hard against a man in a suit, surrounded by four or five big, muscular-looking fellows.

"Excuse me!" Mike snapped and attempted to squeeze past.

But the musclemen wouldn't let him pass. His temper reached boiling point.

"Will you PLEASE get out of my way!" he bellowed at the man in the suit, so annoyed that he didn't really see him.

"Absolutely. Let him pass, boys!" the man ordered. "Hey. You're Mike, aren't you? Mike Rofone?"

Mike stopped dead in his tracks. The man looked awfully familiar... oh no. It couldn't be... it WAS...

"I'm the President," the man said, firmly gripping Mike's hand and pumping it.

"Since you couldn't be here earlier, I decided to come back and give you your award personally. Well done, Mike!"

Now, a huge cheer erupted from the office behind them. Mike looked sheepishly over his shoulder to see Mr Broadhead, Indie and Amy leading the rest in a round of applause for him. He'd been tricked!

"Aw shucks," he managed, blushing furiously.

The President looked at Mike very formally. "Thanks to you and your friends, we've successfully stormed the bunker and our team are investigating the contents now. Viper Virus, Donna and Jason Ratz will pay dearly for what they've done!"

Mike was glad to hear that the mission was successful. But then he saw the President's face grow a little embarrassed.

"Trouble is, we're having a bit of trouble catching Viper."

"What?" Mike was immediately wary. "But I left him in the bunker!"

The President looked more embarrassed. "I know. But my men found nothing."

There was silence for a moment as Mike absorbed this. It seemed that Viper Virus had once again eluded him. He gave a long weary sigh.

The President looked hard at him.

"You looked bushed, Mike. I think you should take a holiday, all expenses paid. By the Government, of course."

Mike immediately cheered up. "Thanks. To tell you the truth, I could do with it. I've had a heck of a day."

The President nodded sympathetically. "Tell me about it. I've had two threatened coups, a couple of minor personal scandals and my car wouldn't start this morning."

Mike patted the President's shoulder. "Wanna talk about it?"

The President looked tempted. "Yeah. Over a milkshake? Nobody knows this, but I got this terrible addiction to milkshakes. I can't beat it, no matter how hard I try."

"Yeah?" Mike said with interest. "Funnily enough, I've just beaten a lifelong addiction to cola."

The President was all ears. "Really? How?"

"Let me get my stuff and I'll tell you all about it."

Mike went back to his desk, grabbed his coat and switched off his computer. He turned to Mr Broadhead. "I think I deserve the rest of the day off."

Mr Broadhead smiled back. "You go right ahead, Mike." Mike winked over his shoulder at Indie and Amy, then chummily took the President's arm and led him off down the corridor. "About your milkshake addiction. Have you tried self-help groups?"

The President shook his head. "It's kind of hard, in my job. If the Press ever got hold of it... you know what scavengers they are."

"Not all of us," Mike said indignantly.

"Hey sorry, I didn't mean to offend you, Mike."

Mike shrugged manfully. "No offence taken."

They turned the corner and disappeared.

Back on Mike's desk, his computer gave a small shudder and suddenly came back to life. Funny green letters shivered eerily on the screen before joining together in a message...

I'll be back. Viper.

A ghostly laugh came from deep in the heart of the computer and then the screen went dead.

OTHER GREAT TITLES FROM BLACKWATER PRESS

£3.99

When Granny decides to kidnap the Taoiseach all hell breaks loose. She only wants to persuade him to make her the next President of Ireland, but with reporters and the gardaí hot on her trail she is fast becoming the country's most famous fugitive!

Once again, the Kett family must join forces to save Granny – but this is easier said than done. Who is the curious character in torn tights who arrives on their doorstep, and how can he help them in their daring mission? And who exactly has Granny managed to abduct in her bid for the presidency – the real Taoiseach, or an imposter with ambitions of his own...?

£3.99

...What animal is taller sitting down than standing up? Who lives at 1600 Pennsylvania Avenue? Can you discover the hidden phrase in ECNALG? Which Egyptian pharoh fathered 162 children? What four-tonne dinosaur had a brain the size of a walnut? Is it possible to slice a banana without removing its skin?... Tax your brain, test your knowledge and trick your friends! *Brainstorm* is crammed with quizzes, jokes, amazing true-life stories, puzzles, facinating facts, riddles and magic tricks.

Indigo

Did you know that Mike Rofone started his life on the Internet with Indigo, Ireland's leading Internet company? Indigo is the home of fun, games and learning and the fastest way to the Internet world.

The Internet is a set of computers which can help you find out about stuff from sports to school subjects and to send messages around the world at the touch of a button.

See our home pages at www.indigo.ie to find fun places like Mike Rofone, the X-Files and Nintendo. Read, see and hear the lastest about your favourite football team or pop group.

Send e-mail to anyone anywhere in the world, from the President of the United States to Santa Claus!

Use our pages to help you with your school project, English essay or geography homework.

Discover the world with Indigo
Phone us now at 1-850-463446